SISTER ON PENHALLOW WARD

It wasn't coincidence that brought Kate Browning to work as ward sister at a hospital in Cornwall—she knew and loved the area and saw it as a haven after the death of her beloved young husband. But to find the surgeon who had been so cruelly jilted by her sister working in the same hospital was more than she had bargained for . . .

Janet Ferguson was born at Newmarket, Suffolk. She nursed as a VAD during the Second World War, then became a medical secretary working in hospitals in London and the provinces and (more latterly) in Brighton, Sussex, where she now lives. She has had eighteen novels published—seven of them being Doctor-Nurse Romances. These, she says, she finds the most satisfying and interesting to plot: 'I couldn't be happy unless I had a story to weave. My characters are nearly as real to me as my friends and colleagues, several of whom are nurses and who—sometimes unwittingly—supply me with the kind of material I can use!'

SISTER ON PENHALLOW WARD

BY

JANET FERGUSON

MILLS & BOON LIMITED
15–16 BROOK'S MEWS
LONDON W1A 1DR

*First published in Great Britain 1986
by Mills & Boon Limited*

© Janet Ferguson 1986

*Australian copyright 1986
Philippine copyright 1986*

ISBN 0 263 75396 4

Set in 10 on 11½ pt Linotron Times
03–0586–54,050

*Photoset by Rowland Phototypesetting Limited
Bury St Edmunds, Suffolk*
*Printed and bound in Great Britain by
Collins, Glasgow*

CHAPTER ONE

'THE CITY HOSPITAL, Tradstow, Cornwall: Due to the retirement of the current post-holder, a vacancy will shortly be arising for a full-time Sister/Charge Nurse on Penhallow, our female surgical ward. Candidates should have had a minimum of three years' post-registration experience.'

Kate saw the advertisement eighteen months after her husband had died. As she read the words a kind of excitement spiralled its way inside her. Now, this might be exactly, but *exactly* what she needed. Clutching her *Nursing Times*, she ran downstairs.

She told her mother and sister, Rose, about it at breakfast-time. 'I'm going to apply, and if I get it I shall live at the cottage,' she said in her quiet but very determined way.

Two pairs of blue eyes regarded her, two pairs of slim brows rose. 'You can't want to live in Cornwall, Katie, it's too far from London!' Rose exclaimed, looking scandalised.

'I don't want to hug London for ever.' Kate reached for the toast. Rose was most likely remembering that Ian Casson had gone to Cornwall. He had moved there nearly two years ago, after Rose had jilted him and married Hugh, who had been his consultant boss.

'Ian went to Tradstow—Hugh told me so. He got a consultant post there,' said Rose, surprising Kate not at all.

'He'll be at the Royal Ear, Nose and Throat Clinic,' Kate pointed out. '*This* job,' she stabbed at her paper, 'is on the other side of Tradstow. I'm very unlikely to run into Ian, and even if I did, I doubt if he's still suffering agonies, Rose, not after all this time. He's probably engaged, or married, or something. He was very chaseable.'

'Sometimes I still feel guilty about him,' sighed Rose.

And so you should, thought Kate, but she didn't say so, for she loved her sister, who was three months pregnant, and over-emotional, and easily upset. Instead she told her in kindly tones—the sort she used on the wards—not to worry, Ian was all in the past.

'You're very unlikely to get the job,' Audrey Christy, their mother, broke in. 'Twenty-five is young for a Ward Sister, and despite what the advert says, they'll be looking for someone in their thirties, ten years older than you.'

'I intend to apply. If I don't do that I won't even be in with a chance.' Kate was used to her mother's cold-water tactics, and they didn't bother her much. Audrey Christy had divorced her Cornish husband when her daughters were twelve and thirteen. She was a cool, clever, academic type—a partner in the firm of Jules and Christy, solicitors in the town.

'It's the cottage pulling at you, of course. You're dying to live there, I know.' Her glance went to Kate and then to her watch; she had an early appointment. Even so she delayed a little, looking across at her daughters—at Rose, the elder, who was delicate, fair-haired like herself, married to Professor Hugh Clevington, consultant ENT surgeon at the Walbrook Hospital, London, near St Paul's. Rose was home for the weekend while her husband was away; she and Hugh had a house on Highgate Hill. Kate lived at home, she had done so since her young husband, Daniel, had died. She was a staff nurse at the County Hospital, and she drove to work each day in the yellow Fiat that had once belonged to Dan. Kate was the strong one—strong-featured, strong-willed, resolute in a crisis. Her presence lent a sense of security. Kate was so supportive; in no way did her mother want her to go.

'I have to admit,' Kate was saying, 'that I would love to live at the cottage. Poldenack Bay is only four miles out of Tradstow itself. I could drive to and from the hospital, the same as I do here. You knew I would leave Surrey some time, Mother; we've discussed it, haven't we?'

'Apply if you must,' Audrey Christy frowned, as she slid into her jacket and picked up her shoulder-bag from a nearby chair, 'but you won't get it, Kate my darling, they'll want someone older. You won't stand a chance, you'll only be wasting your time.'

She was wrong, for Kate was awarded the post, and she started work on Penhallow Ward in mid-April, when Cornwall was decked for spring. And it seemed as though the move had been right, for, as Kate put it herself, everything was to her liking, she couldn't see any snags. The post was a highly responsible one, which stretched her to full potential; it made full use of her training and experience, her inherent talent for nursing, her gift for caring, her passion for making well. The staff liked her, so did the patients, and the cottage at Poldenack Bay, left to her four years ago by her Cornish grandmother, received her into its shabby arms; Aubyns Cottage had been let to various tenants who hadn't treated it well. What a good thing I like decorating, she thought when she walked in. One of her hobbies was wielding brushfuls of paint. Then suddenly, six weeks later, the unexpected happened . . .

And nothing was ever quite the same again.

The fateful day, a Wednesday, began the same as usual, with Kate doing her round of the ward, distributing patients' mail, and listening to one or two tales of woe which were whispered into her ear. Mr Jarman, the general surgeon, and his houseman, Derek Coles, saw four post-operative patients and two recent admissions, and spoke to three others being discharged. At lunchtime, up in the staff cafeteria, Kate sat with Oliver Brady, the charge nurse on Fratton Ward, which was male surgical. Oliver Brady, 'Olly' to his friends, was large and avuncular. He was a widower in his early fifties, who looked like Friar Tuck; and right from the first he had taken Kate under his wing. Olly was given to prophecies, he was superstitious too. Kate rarely took his forecasts seriously, although she was forced to admit that one or two of them *had* been known to come true.

'I don't want to alarm you, Kathryn,' he said, over their second course, 'but I have a feeling that some sort of change is about to be sprung on us.'

'On you and me?'

He nodded, eating his ice-cream and prunes, spectacles lying folded by his plate. He always removed his glasses whenever he ate or drank; it was one of his many idiosyncrasies.

'Whatever change we're in for, I expect we'll cope,' said Kate, screwing up her paper napkin and getting to her feet. 'I'll have to be getting back, Olly—we're short-staffed, as usual. The SNO promised me temporary help, but so far, nothing doing.' She left him wagging his balding head, still glooming on troubles to come, and ran downstairs, not waiting for the lift.

It was the patients' quiet time when she got back to the ward, the rest time just after lunch, before the start of visiting. It was early June, and beyond the long, old-fashioned windows, the Cornish summer was under way, the sun was bearing power. Four miles to the west the rumbustious Atlantic, tamed to sheet blue satin, was creaming itself in foam on shore and rocks.

Kate scanned the ward as she stood by the doors, her eye alighting briefly on Learner Nurse Solly at the central desk, on Nurse Heston opening a window, on Staff Nurse True handing pale pink knitting back to Mrs Vane, on Zia, the domestic, sponging milk from the floor. Apart from one or two sniffs and clearings, and the footfalls of the nurses, there was a hushy silence, and an overall tidiness, and only one vacant bed. This belonged to Mrs Proudman, who was on her way back to it, walking slowly and carefully, due to her stitches; she had had an appendicectomy. Kate went to meet her, putting an arm round her waist. 'Try to hold yourself straighter,' she counselled, 'don't bend over your wound.' Mrs Proudman grunted, but did as she said and, entwined, they reached her bed. Kate sat her on it and removed her mules, lifting her legs with care; she covered her up and straightened the candlewick spread. 'I expect those few yards felt like miles!'

Mrs Proudman mopped her face. 'They did, Sister, and bed feels like heaven. You won't get me out again, not until after supper, not even if I burst!'

Kate laughed. 'Rest now, till your husband comes.'

'Yes, he told me he'd be along. He's got time off specially—he's a good one, is my Don. You're married, I see.' She had noticed the plain gold ring on Kate's left hand.

'I'm a widow,' Kate said shortly, feeling a waft of sadness that came and passed, touching her like a ghost. She moved away from Mrs Proudman, rebutting further enquiries, and went to her office just outside the ward doors.

It was a small room with glass on two sides; one side

looked into the ward, the other on to the teeming city from four floors up. In the near distance was Tradstow Cathedral, rising in gothic splendour high above the shops and offices and municipal buildings, its towers and pinnacles reaching for the sky. The slatted blind made stripes on Kate's slim-fitting Sister's dress, it zebraed her hair, which was glossy and brown, and taken up into a knot. It even contrived to put in the shade her white muslin cap, light as a snowflake and trimmed with bands of lace. All this she could see in the wall mirror, and then she became aware that the up-and-down wail of ambulance sirens—almost a background sound to those who work in hospitals—had been going on for some time. It must be an accident pile-up, she thought; Casualty will be busy. She moved to her desk just as the telephone rang:

'Penhallow Ward, Sister Browning speaking.' She had hardly announced herself before the incisive voice of the Senior Nursing Officer, Miss Angela Rone, came piercingly into her ear.

'Sister Browning, a juggernaut lorry has crashed into the Outpatients' Wing of the Royal ENT Clinic on Tolcanbury Hill. The Department was empty, as it was Wednesday, which was nothing short of miraculous, but the two wards above have been rendered unsafe, patients are being transferred to other parts of the Clinic, and to us as an overspill. Now, can you make room for four female patients in your ward? One is a child, post-tonsillectomy, the other three are adults —one a mastoidectomy, I think; I have few details as yet.'

'Four patients . . . into Penhallow . . . how soon . . . when will they come?' The receiver slipped in Kate's grasp, as the SNO carried on:

'Within the hour, so I'm told, and I see from the

bed-list, Sister, that both your side-wards are free at the moment. You must make use of those.'

'There's room for two beds in each, with a squeeze. So yes, Miss Rone, I can manage.' After the first bolting shock Kate's mind slid into gear and began to plan with calm speed for this unforeseen insurgence. Somewhere around in the wash of her thoughts were queries about Ian Casson. She knew he was at the ENT Clinic, so were the patients his? Had he been hurt? She knew him, so it was reasonable to ask: 'You said no patients were hurt, Miss Rone, but are the staff all right?' As she asked the question her mind's eyes sharpened, and she saw in graphic detail the picture of an enormous lorry hopelessly out of control, ploughing and plunging into the building, tunnelling into one wing. A frisson of horror made her back go cold.

Miss Rone didn't reply at once, she was too busy giving instructions. 'All right then, Sister, over to you, make preparations at once. Get anything you want sent up from Stores and Central Sterile Supply. I might add that you've taken the news more calmly than Charge Nurse Brady,' she added. 'In addition to five overspill patients, he's likely to have to admit the driver of the lorry into Fratton Ward. He—the driver—has chest injuries, and is in our theatre now. As to anyone other than he being hurt, by the grace of God no one was—at least not seriously. There were cuts from flying glass, minor injuries from falling timbers, and then there would be shock—the shock must have been appalling!' Miss Rone paused for breath at this point. 'All right then, Sister, thank you, that's all. I'll leave you to get on.' Her phone went down, and replacing her own, Kate went into action. From the ward doors she beckoned to Staff Nurse True.

Extra beds and bedding were ordered, lockers and

bedside trays. The clinical room next to Kate's office yielded up dishes and bowls, tracheostomy apparatus, forceps and catheters; further dressings were sent up from Central Supply. 'Until we know what we're in for, best to be prepared,' Staff Nurse True remarked, making a bedclothes pack with her eye on Nurse Solly, who was dragging in two commodes.

'Short-staffed as we are, let's hope the patients will all be walking ones,' said Kate, as she stood in the doorway of the first of the two side-wards, checking items off a foolscap list. 'And I've had second thoughts about the child tonsillectomy. Staff. I'm going to put her in the main ward, and bring Mrs Proudman in here. Mrs Proudman won't mind, and the child will be better where there's more for her to see. Not only that, but the ear patient will appreciate quietness. Margaret Proudman's not a garrulous type, she reads most of the time.'

'I think you're right.' Joan True, who was twice Kate's age, blew a strand of hair from her eyes and rubbed the small of her back. 'We'll just swap beds around, shall we . . . wheel Mrs Proudman's in, and this one out?' She began to jerk at the first of the newly-made beds, signalling to Nurse Solly to lend a hand.

Minutes later, back they came with Mrs Proudman's bed, she trailing behind it, clutching her abdomen. 'I couldn't just lie in it, could I, and let them lug me along?' she said wearily, clutching her abdomen. But her face brightened when she saw the side-ward. 'Oh, I like it, Sister, it's great! Now all I need,' her green eyes shone —Mrs Proudman was a redhead—'is a dishy man to go in the other bed!'

'Sorry we can't oblige,' laughed Kate, remembering to tell Nurse Solly to make quite sure Mr Donald Proudman was told where his wife was. 'Don't let him go into the main ward and find she's no longer there. There's nothing more alarming than that to layman visitors; somehow or other they always think the worst.'

'I'll see to it, Sister, I'll catch him as he comes across from the lifts.' Learner Nurse Solly closed the side-ward door.

Seconds later, so it seemed to Kate, the refugee patients arrived—two in wheelchairs, two on stretchers, labels pinned to their sleeves. The little girl, with her mother walking alongside her chair, was wheeled into the main ward and helped into bed. The ear patient joined Mrs Proudman, while a spiky-haired young woman, whose label simply said, 'bruised larynx, in for observation', was put into the second side-ward with a sinusitis patient. Kate visited all four of them, listening to their accounts of the earthquake shaking-up they had felt when the great lorry struck. 'I thought it was a bomb,' Jane Clifford, the mastoidectomy, said, 'but I expect having this,' her hand went up to her wadded ear, 'I'm apt to be extra sensitive to noise.'

'You'll be quiet enough in here, love,' Mrs Proudman told her, 'we don't have anything bashing us . . . don't allow it, do we, Sister?'

'Absolutely not,' Kate agreed, backing out into the corridor. Having two beds in a single room left scant room for manoeuvre. And the corridor was even more space-invaded, being thronged with visitors. One man stood out from all the rest; he was trying to weave his way through. He was tall, or tallish, he was fair-haired, and Kate recognised him at once. Even with such a restricted view, hemmed in as he was by the crowd, she knew him. It was Ian Casson—lean-faced and looking impatient. He caught her glance, and she saw his jaw go slack. In no time they were face-to-face, Miss Rone at his side; she introduced the two of them before they could say a word. Kate was aware of Ian's hand tight and hard round hers. As it fell to his side, he said with a smile: 'Mrs Browning and I, Miss Rone, are already acquainted—I know her family well.'

'I didn't know that!' Miss Rone was surprised, and she darted a look at Kate. 'Well, I'll leave you in her very good hands.' Still looking rather surprised, she made her way through the crowd to the landing outside.

Kate, under Ian's scrutiny, tried to look unconcerned. 'How astonishing to find you in Cornwall, Kate.' There was something in his voice—dismay, perhaps, that made her speak up for herself.

'I wanted this job.' The palms of her hands met the cool of the wall behind. Meeting his eyes was terrible, for instinctively she felt that coming upon her so suddenly hadn't pleased him very much. Seeing her brought the past back, of course, touched on old scars, and however well those scars had healed, they were sensitive areas. He seemed different, so aloof and haughty. She observed the lift to his chin. He would hate and loathe and abominate being reminded of past mistakes. He would rather I weren't here, she thought, but I am, and I can't disappear. He'll have to put up with the situation in the same way that I will. *I* don't like it either, it makes for embarrassment, one of the most uncomfortable feelings there is.

'Congratulations on landing the job, I'm sure you suit it well.' A careful smile moved his mouth but didn't reach his eyes. 'Perhaps I could see my patients now —the little girl first, I think.'

'Of course, sir.' The formal title set suitable distance between them. It emphasised rank, made their respective roles plain. 'I put Emily in the main ward,' she told him, 'I thought she'd be happier there. Mr Jarman's patient, Mrs Proudman, is in the side-ward with your Miss Clifford.'

'I'm obliged, thank you,' was all he said, but she felt he wasn't displeased. Moving away, she preceded him into the ward.

Emily Fawley, eight years old, on her second post-operative day, was lying propped up, holding her mother's hand. Her pale, peaky little face, curtained in rich dark hair, brightened when she saw the surgeon. 'I knew you'd come,' she croaked.

'I promised I would, remember?' His smile, now, was unreserved. 'It was rather an exciting adventure, wasn't it? I escaped too, you see. I had to, to look after you—I followed your ambulance.'

'It was all so . . . *dreadful*!' The mother gave a shudder. 'When can I have her home, Mr Casson? I shan't rest easy, not till she's home and sleeping in her own bed.'

He spoke reassuringly to her, and as Kate stood by the bed, Staff Nurse True came in with Emily's notes. 'They've just come.' She looked at Kate, but gave the notes to Ian Casson; she felt she couldn't ignore his outstretched hand. He asked her to bring an auriscope.

'And some spatulas,' he added, 'and perhaps you would take Mrs Fawley into the waiting-room. I'll see you again in a minute, Mrs Fawley, but I want to examine Emily. I take up rather a lot of room.' Kate was curtaining the bed-space, and Mrs Fawley followed Staff Nurse out of the ward.

As well as looking down Emily's throat, he examined both her ears, for any possible reddening of the drums. 'So far so good,' he said, as he walked with Kate to the desk. 'Give her an aspirin mixture to be gargled and swallowed before her meals. Keep her food items soft for the moment. Encourage her to swallow . . . the more she does, the easier it will become.'

'Yes, sir,' said Kate, watching him write in the notes. His head was bent and she found herself staring at his tough fair hair, thick and unshiny, springing away from the crown.

'You'll have nursed ENT patients before.' His remark wasn't quite a question, yet it wasn't entirely a statement, either; it lay between the two. Again she felt she had to speak up for herself.

'I have, yes, many times,' she told him quietly, 'and I've always found that branch of nursing especially interesting.'

'I'm glad to hear it.' He straightened up. 'Emily's doing well. I can probably discharge her on Friday, which should lighten your load a little. It can't have been easy to have to take in . . .' He stopped and spun round on his heel. So did Kate, for she had heard what he had—a blunted crashing sound, the muffled thud of a body hitting the ground.

There were cries from all sides, chairs scraping back, one of them overturned. There, on the floor, not three feet from Emily Fawley's bed, lay the heaped-up form of a man in blazer and slacks. 'Mr Proudman!' Kate jerked out the name, as she ran swiftly forward, Ian beside her; he reached the unconscious man first.

'Just a faint, I think.' He turned Mr Proudman's greying head to the side, and felt for the big artery in his neck. 'There's a good pulse, let's get him out,' he said, just as Mrs Fawley re-entered the ward and gave a piercing shriek. Ian moved behind Mr Proudman's head, hooked his hands under his armpits, then walking backwards he slithered him along, swiftly and all but noiselessly, over the vinyl, towards the ward doors, and out.

In the passage they turned him on to his side, his head in Kate's lap. 'He's coming to already,' said Ian. 'It's as I thought, a faint. If you've any ammonium carbonate that should speed things up even more.' Nurse Heston, a second-year student, was already bringing some.

'I thought . . .' she held the phial out to Kate.

'You thought right.' Kate unscrewed the top, and very soon Donald Proudman was sitting up. 'But don't try to stand, not yet,' Kate advised, 'not till you're perfectly steady. Your wife is quite all right, you know. She's just been moved, that's all. We've put her into one of the side-wards . . . no, not because she's worse. It's a little re-shuffle we've had to make. Mrs Proudman is doing splendidly. In a minute or two you can go in and see for yourself.'

He looked at Kate with dazed eyes. 'Never fainted before in my life,' he muttered.

'I'm sorry about it . . . it's a horrid feeling.' His colour was coming back, and Kate let out her breath as she helped him to his feet. 'And you're quite sure Maggie's all right, Sister?'

'Yes, I'm positive.' They exchanged smiles, and she held his arm while Nurse Heston fetched a chair; he sat down, looking anxiously up at Kate.

'I'd rather you didn't tell her I passed out like that. She'll only worry, think I've not been feeding myself as I should.' Or that we're incompetent, Kate thought, feeling vexed. Ian Casson had long since left them, but she knew he was in her room. Through the open doorway she could see a long shadow falling across the carpet, she could hear his voice; he was speaking on the phone.

Presently Donald Proudman went in to see his wife. Not a word was said about his collapse, but as Kate closed the side-ward door, she heard Margaret Proudman telling him off about the dust on his blazer.

'Honestly, Don, you look as though you've been rolling about on the floor!'

Why, oh why, Kate wondered, hadn't Nurse Solly waylaid him, intercepted him, stopped him going into the ward? She knew him, she had seen him before, but perhaps there was some excuse—all those visitors coming so quickly, and Mr Proudman was small. Even so, the girl would have to be told. Kate hated reprimanding people; she could do it, but hated the task. It's my weakness, she thought, my Achilles heel. I must make sure it doesn't show. Sighing a little, she went into the office and joined Ian Casson, who stared at her as though she'd no right to be there. 'How is he?' he demanded.

'He's with his wife. Thank you for helping me.'

'It might have been better, don't you think,' his fingertips trailed the desk, 'if someone had thought to warn him that his wife had been transferred? A shock like that, to a man of his age, might have had serious consequences. Excuse me . . .' the phone was ringing, 'I put a call through to my house. My secretary promised to ring me back. This will be her now.'

He had made himself at home in her room, and Kate watched him pick up the phone. 'Yes, Miss Latham— yes, that's the one, read it to me, will you? Pad, please.' He gestured to Kate, who gave him a jotter and pencil, and a cool stare. And then she left the room.

She left it feeling distinctly huffed. What a cheek the man had got . . . criticising, making free with her phone, snapping his fingers—well, almost snapping them—for something to scribble on! He ought to be good and grateful that his patients had been taken in. Had he no idea of all the hassle entailed?

She was being unfair, she knew she was; he couldn't help what had happened. In a bid to drown her unworthy

feelings, she stepped across to the kitchen and poured
herself some tea from the trolley urn. It was three-thirty,
and the giant clock on the west side of the cathedral
chimed the half-hour in the manner of Big Ben. As the
sound died away another, much smaller one made her
strain her ears. She knew what it was—the ting of the
telephone going back on to its rest. So Ian must have
finished, which meant she must join him; swiftly she
crossed the kitchen. They met in the corridor, Ian
looking haggard and drawn.

'Ian!' His Christian name came without thinking as
concern and compunction smote her. He must be having
a ghastly time . . . what had happened was taking its
toll—the business of the crash, his patients at risk, the
absolute shock of it all. 'Let me get you some tea. Sit
down and rest . . . you're looking all in, you know!'

'Don't worry, I shan't swoon on you, Kate.' The smile
she remembered came out and rucked his face, she
found herself smiling back. 'Tea sounds inviting,' he
said, 'but I mustn't stop for it. There's a heck of a lot of
rearranging to be seen to at the Clinic. I live just
opposite, over my consulting rooms. I saw the lorry
careering down the hill, and I knew it was going to crash;
the Outpatients' Wing just sat there, waiting. I think I
closed my eyes!'

'It must have been awful,' Kate responded, aware of
his change of manner. This was more like the man she
had known when he and Rose had been engaged, the
man who had nearly become her brother-in-law. She
might have said more about the crash, but a visitor from
the ward was trying to attract her attention. She turned
to speak to him, then heard Ian say at her back:

'Look, Sister, you carry on. I can find my way to the
side-wards. I've been here before, you know.'

'I can't let you do that!' Her voice rang in protest, for

no one let consultants wander about all on their own; they had to be waited upon.

'Nonsense!' He sounded amused. 'Oh, here's Staff Nurse, she'll deal with me. You carry on with your usual tasks, I've wasted enough of your time.'

'I would hardly say wasted,' she protested again, but she spoke to the empty air. Already he and a plainly flattered Staff Nurse True were opening the first of the side-wards and going inside.

Kate dealt with the visitor's enquiry, and with several others besides. Then the hospital chaplain wanted a word, while one of the physiotherapists called to discuss an exercise programme for a chest surgery patient. After that Miss Gill, the phlebotomist, came to take one or two samples. Once she had gone, bearing her bottles and labels and filled-up forms, visiting time was over and done and the ward was settling down. Ambulant patients were shuffling out to the bathrooms and toilets, while nurses were plunging flowers into bowls.

Ian had gone, so Staff Nurse told Kate: 'He said into Fratton Ward.' But when Olly came in later on, flushed and flurried and hot, it was to tell her that 'sir' had gone down to theatre block. 'The lorry driver's in the recovery room, Mr Casson wanted to see him. Once his condition has stabilised he'll be brought up here to me. Oh dear, Kathryn, what a terrible time, what an afternoon it's been! What did I tell you? I knew there was something. I felt it coming on!' Wiping his forehead, Olly went back to his ward.

Kate watched him go, swaybacked and large, rocking as he walked, trousers dark beneath his Kildare coat. She knew that for all his appearance of flap, Olly was inwardly calm. He was well in command of the situation, he was solidly competent—a first-class nurse who never spared himself.

An hour later she went off duty and made her way out to her car. She was crossing the tarmac when a girl in a van, with HELEN'S FLOWERS on the side, hailed her from the driving seat, then opened the door and jumped down. She ran towards Kate—a flying figure in a blue skirt and sleeveless top, a scarlet bandeau straining back her hair. 'Nurse! Oh, sorry . . . Sister!' she saw the badge on Kate's breast, 'I've just come by the ENT Clinic and seen the state it's in. I asked about Mr Casson, the surgeon, and they told me he was all right. They said he was here,' she looked very anxious, 'but no one had time to explain. Why is he here, if he's not hurt? Have you seen him, by any chance? Is he in Cas?' She stared across the yard.

'He's not hurt at all,' Kate assured her. 'He came here with some of his patients. He's in the building, getting them settled down.'

'Oh, is *that* it! Oh, thank goodness!' The girl let out a 'phew!' of relief. The breeze moved her hair, which was short and curly, over the top of the bandeau. 'Will he be long?' She smiled charmingly at Kate.

'I don't know. I can't tell you that.' Kate turned to unlock the Fiat. She slid behind the steering wheel, hoping the girl would go. She was young and fresh and sweetly pretty, and she made Kate feel about ninety . . . at *least* ninety . . . her head was beginning to ache.

'I'll go and find his car and squat—that way I can't miss him!' With a little laugh and a flash of gold bracelets —the thin, tinkling kind—the girl stood away to allow Kate to drive off. She waved, Kate could see her in the mirror, a sliver of bright colour on the dull tarmac, like a brilliant dragonfly.

A girl-friend of Ian's, that's obvious, she thought as she crawled through the city in the evening rush-hour, driving against the sun. Was she special, or just one of several? He was a very attractive man; he had presence, distinction, a powerful toughness . . . in itself a kind of allure. Rose had always seemed too fragile for a man of his calibre. And yet . . . and yet . . . he was plainly attracted to the type of girl Rose was—the little delicate gauzy type, like the one now waiting for him, spreading her skirts on the bonnet of his car.

Perhaps he'll have more luck with this one. A wave of self-disdain broke in Kate; she felt disturbed, very un-like herself. And her mood stayed with her till she reached the coast, till she reached Poldenack Bay, till she saw the sea with its crusting of diamonds, till she forced the car up the hill—up and away from the little harbour, up to the two stone cottages, to her own, which was Aubyns, and to Pinnocks, the one next door.

CHAPTER TWO

THE cottages were set very close together, and their gardens abutted, a hedge of cupressus dividing them like a wall. There was someone living at Pinnocks who typed— a tall narrow man, with drifty hair and blue-jeaned legs; Kate had seen him in the garden through a thin part of the hedge, one afternoon.

As she slowed past his cottage this evening to make the turn into her drive, she saw him standing at his open window; she got a good look at his face for the first time, and recollection stirred. Unless she was much mistaken her neighbour was Ellis Rand—the man whose first book had been a bestseller; she had seen him on television, and there had been something about him in her weekly magazine. Had she kept the magazine? Surely she must have, she couldn't have thrown it away. As soon as she got in she searched for and found it—and yes, it was him! There he was on the centre pages, posed at his writing desk, looking selfconscious, and holding his bestseller book.

Kate read the feature carefully, missing not one word. He was thirty-one, unattached, had given up his job as a book buyer in a London store to try his hand at a novel. He had lived on his savings for two years while he was writing the book. Then he had found an agent who placed it for him, it had come out in the New Year, and half a million copies had been sold. It was to be televised in the winter; it was called *Bland Justice*, and naturally its author was very pleased. The feature concluded by saying that Ellis Rand lived in Whitechapel in a pied-à-terre near the London Hospital.

Kate laid the magazine on the sink-top while she delved into the fridge for cheese and salad—a simple meal she could take out into the garden. But an author next door . . . how exciting! She began to slice tomatoes, still glancing over at the open magazine. Of course he wasn't exactly famous, or at least he wasn't yet, but he must be very clever to have written a bestseller. Her father would be interested, she must remember to tell him about it. Anything in the creative line—John Christy was an actor—always grabbed him; Kate wrote to him every month.

When she heard the garden gate open and close, when she looked through the kitchen window and saw Ellis Rand coming up the path, the day had been so extra-ordinary, and so unreal, that she wasn't very surprised. He went to the front door round at the side, using her new brass knocker shaped like a dolphin, making the merest tap. Putting down a bunch of wet lettuce and drying her hands on her hips, Kate crossed the small hall. Whatever could he want?

She opened the door and there he was, fine dark hair adrift, face square-featured, the rest of him long and thin. 'I'm sorry to bother you like this,' he began before she could speak, 'but I've nicked my finger on the breadknife . . . a careless thing to do. It's only a super-ficial cut, but I can't stop it bleeding. I wondered if you might possibly have a strip of Elastoplast—I can't type with an ordinary bandage.' He held up his left fore-finger, swathed in a handkerchief tissue fast turning red. 'The shops are shut, or I wouldn't have worried you.'

'Please come in, Mr Rand.' As she used his name Kate wondered if this was the right thing to do. It might just be his writing name, not his proper one. 'Come through into the kitchen,' she added, 'I keep a first-aid box in there. As yet I've not used it, but I'm sure it will have what we want.'

'You're a nurse, aren't you?' he asked, as she opened the first-aid box. It had been given to her as a 'fun' gift, amongst the more glamorous ones she had had from the Surrey hospital when she left.

'I'm a Ward Sister at the City Hospital,' she told him.

'I thought you probably were.' He watched her unwind the unwieldy dressing, examine the small cut, clean it up and apply a steri-strip. He noticed the wedding ring on her finger, observing her deft movements—gentle, unfussy. She clipped the steri-strip close.

'That should be all right, I think. It's unlikely to bleed any more. The strip should hold it nicely, and you should be able to type. I'm Kate Browning, by the way,' she smiled as she closed the box.

'I'm Ellis Rand—but I see you know that. You've been checking up on me.' He looked at the opened magazine still lying on the draining-board, flanked by sliced tomatoes and lettuce and cheese.

'Guilty!' she admitted, and was glad to see that he knew how to smile. 'When I saw you at your window just now I knew I'd seen your photograph, and I thought I knew where; I came in and looked you up. I guessed you were a writer, anyway; I can hear your machine at night.'

'Does it disturb you?' He looked anxious again, his brown eyes had very clear whites. He isn't handsome, but I like his looks, she decided as she assured him that his typewriter rattle didn't bother her at all. 'I'm glad about that,' he said earnestly, 'because I'm here till the end of the summer, and I may stay longer; my new novel is being set in these parts. You look very well settled in, Mrs Browning.' His glance, and he didn't miss much, travelled round the little kitchen with its newly painted walls, and the modern fitments which Kate had had installed. It was very different from the one next door, which looked much as hers had done two months ago, when she had first moved in.

'I *am* settled,' she emphasised. 'Aubyns is my home —I own it, I'm here for always. I've recently moved from Surrey. I think we probably came here at roughly the same time.'

'Yes, I think we did.' He got to his feet. 'I'll go out this way, shall I? Thank you again for the first-aid.' He opened the kitchen door, then, turning to smile just briefly, and raising his hand in farewell, he walked down the path with loping strides, his mind already grappling with the fourth, very difficult chapter of his book.

Kate awoke in the night, in the small hours, and heard his typewriter going. The windows of the two cottages were open, and the volley-bursts of sound made a strident contrast to the ever-present hiss and roll of the sea. As she lay there in the darkness, watching the bedroom curtains trying to bend themselves out of the window, her thoughts returned to the ward—to the scene with Ian that afternoon, then back to an earlier one which had played itself out two and a half years ago. It had been when Rose had rung her up, very late one night, to tell her that her engagement to Ian was off.

'I'm going to marry Hugh, Katie. I love him and he loves me. It's been happening gradually for some weeks now. I just couldn't help myself.'

It had been several seconds before Kate, startled by Rose's news, could gather herself sufficiently to remember who Hugh was. Rose soon enlightened her, sounding exasperated: '*Professor* Hugh Clevington, you dimwit! The consultant I'm secretary to! Oh, wake up, Katie, you're half asleep . . . can't you take it in?'

'Tell her to ring at a civilised hour,' Danny had growled beside Kate, but she shut him up.

'Rose, what are you saying! The Professor is Ian's chief! And he's years and years older than you! You can't possibly do such a thing!'

'He's eighteen years older than me, which makes him forty-two. If he were fifty years older I would still want him. He's right for me, don't you see?'

Kate hadn't seen, she had been upset. 'But what about Ian?' she cried.

'He's furious, but he'll get over it,' Rose said awkwardly. 'These things happen—I've not committed a crime.'

She married the Professor six months later, but by then Ian Casson had secured his consultant post in Tradstow and moved out of reach. Kate often wondered how he was getting on.

During his three months' engagement to Rose, she and Danny had met him probably half a dozen times when they made up a four, or met at the Surrey house en famille. Ian remarked on how unalike the two sisters were, and Danny said: 'Good job too,' under his breath, of course. Considering himself a good judge of women, he had dubbed Rose a cold little fish. Privately he wished Ian joy of her, and when the break-up came, he told Kate he had had a lucky escape.

'That depends on how much he loves her,' said Kate. She hardly thought Ian Casson was the type to fall out of love that easily. At the time she had thought Rose callous—she had gone behind Ian's back, she hadn't been straight, and neither had Hugh, which must have been very hurtful. Ian had practically revered his chief —Rose had told her that; he had been his Registrar for four whole years.

Yet now, with the benefit of distance and hindsight,

she thought she could understand what had motivated Rose, and why she had fallen for Hugh. She had been looking for a father figure, which Ian didn't fit. In a way she missed Pa more than I did, Kate thought. Her gaze came back to the curtains shifting and drifting against the windowsill. She's happy with Hugh, one has only to see them together to realise that. She's spoiled, and cherished and cosseted, even more so now she's pregnant. I would loathe that cottonwool kind of loving, but for Rose it's exactly right. We're very different—and this, of course, brought her round full circle to Ian's remark that the two of them weren't alike.

Three of Mr Jarman's patients went down to theatres next day. Ian Casson rang up to say he would be along in the afternoon. Nurse Heston took the telephone call and relayed it to Kate, who was hurrying off to see the SNO. Miss Rone wanted to thank her for her efforts of yesterday. She then went on to tell her there had been a meeting that morning . . . 'At which, Sister Browning, the management team unanimously decided that we must continue to help the ENT Clinic for some considerable time. The Royal is a very old hospital, albeit a very good one, but apart from what happened yesterday, extensive repairs, one might almost say major rebuilding work, is long overdue. Now they want to start it, do the lot at once, in one fell swoop, as one might say.' Miss Rone fussed with her papers, looking mildly irritated. It was all very well for the powers that be to hold out these helping hands, but her wards were chronically short-staffed, especially the surgical ones. 'They—the ENT Clinic,' she went on testily, 'don't want to postpone too many admissions, nor lengthen their surgical lists. *Most* patients will still go there, others will come here. Mr Casson and his Registrar will have the use of one of our theatres for three or four months, depending on how things go. This means that you and Charge Nurse Brady will have patients of Mr Casson's, on and off, all throughout that time.'

'I see.' Kate tried to look unperturbed.

Miss Rone smiled up at her: 'You'll have to deal with two separate consultants' rounds, of course, but that's not very unusual in large wards these days.'

Kate agreed that it wasn't, and said she could manage. 'I shall find it interesting.' But she went up to lunch with very mixed feelings indeed.

'Of course,' Olly said solemnly, for he too had seen Miss Rone, 'it's right that we should lend a hand to the ENT Hospital. Mr Casson has done sterling work for us here on occasion. He's come along many a time, often at weekends, to help out with accident cases involving his special skills.'

'Good of him!' said Kate drily.

Olly looked surprised. 'Don't you like him, Kathryn?'

She flushed. 'Oh yes, I like him all right, but I think he could be . . . trying. I think he could be domineering, he's very confident.' She recalled the way he had been yesterday with Mr Donald Proudman—helpful, yes, but he hadn't forgotten to criticise afterwards, and he'd used her office as though it were his own.

'He's bound to have to be confident,' Olly's tone was reproachful. 'When you're slicing into someone's throat, or burring out an ear, you've got to know what you're doing . . . fumbling might mean curtains. Mr Casson is a very positive kind of man.'

'I'm sure you're right,' Kate said drily.

'And he's very much in demand. He takes private patients too, you know; his rooms are near the Clinic. He's young for it, he can't be very much more than thirty-five.'

Thirty-five was his age exactly, Kate knew that for a fact, and yes, it was young for a surgeon of his rank. 'I should imagine he would be popular.' She kept her eyes on her plate as she weighed up the pros and cons of telling Charge Nurse Brady that she had known Ian Casson long before yesterday. In the end she decided not to; instead she mentioned the girl—the girl in the flower van. Olly might know her. He did, and expounded at length.

'Her name is Reever—Helen Reever. She has her own florist's shop, a sizeable one, with a small staff, along in Quayside Road. Her father set her up in business, he's a very wealthy man—chairman of Pelapas Chemicals. He and the girl's mother live in Boston, Massachusetts, but they have a house in Hampstead, and are over here in England quite a lot. I know all this through my friends the Carruthers; I go to their dinner parties.' Olly smiled and preened himself; he was proud of his social connections. 'The Carruthers,' he went on, 'are related to the Reevers—some sort of cousins, I think. They say Helen is a first-class businesswoman, is shrewd and on the ball. She's often here delivering flowers, likes to bring them right up to the wards. She's not unlike a flower herself . . . colourful and fresh.'

'Yes,' said Kate, 'I thought that yesterday, when I saw her in the yard.' She pushed back her chair. 'I must go, Olly—duty calls, as they say. I've still got another patient to come up from theatres. Oh, by the way, how's the lorry driver, the one who ploughed into the Clinic?'

Olly pursed his lips and looked serious. 'He's been moved to Intensive Care. He has chest and upper abdominal injuries, involving the pancreas. His girl-friend is staying in the hospital, she's with him most of the time.'

'Oh dear, I don't like the sound of that.'

'No, neither do I. *If* he improves, and I do say 'if', he will come up to me, of course. We're supposed to be getting extra help—a nurse from the agency, just one, to share between us, if Miss Rone keeps to her word. The trouble is our SNO's promises are very often pie-crust.' Olly surveyed the flaccid pastry on his apricot pie with disfavour. Leaving him to it, Kate returned to her ward.

She had time, during the quiet hour, to speak with Ian's four patients. The spiky-haired girl with the bruised throat announced that she was all right. She was going, she said, to discharge herself, she was fed-up with hospitals. Kate persuaded her to hang on till Ian had been: 'It'll only be a matter of an hour, Miss Jeeves.' The girl's answer was unrepeatable. Nevertheless, to Kate's relief, she didn't demand her clothes, nor say any more about walking out. Her room-mate, Anne Tremaine, the sinusitis patient, whispered to Kate, when she went to the bathrooms, that Miss Jeeves' bark was worse than her bite.

'Underneath all that brash overlay, Sister, she's really very nice. You can't always judge by appearances and swear-words. I think she just likes to shock.'

'But nursing staff in hospitals don't shock easily,' laughed Kate, and Anne Tremaine joined in.

'I'll examine her in the treatment room,' Ian Casson said, when Kate told him about Miss Jeeves, as soon as he arrived. She had laid out a white coat for him, which he might or might not wear. Consultants could please themselves about coats, but she saw him slip it on. 'Thanks,' he said, as he buttoned it, 'I like to be covered up.' He was more relaxed this afternoon, she noted with relief. She took Miss Jeeves through into the treatment room.

'Head well back, mouth open wide.' He made sure she was comfortable in the chair with a neck rest which Staff

Nurse True had managed to filch from Stores.

Kate warmed a tiny circular mirror in the flame of a spirit lamp. The warming was to stop it steaming up when it met the patient's breath. Testing it on the back of his hand, Ian held it inside her mouth, slightly above the epiglottis, getting a view of her larynx. Eventually he straightened and smiled at her. 'All right, close up, Miss Jeeves. The swelling is much reduced, you're lucky . . . you've not spat any more blood?'

'Not since it happened, no, Doc.'

'Much pain when you speak?'

'No.'

'Well, I think we can let you go home.' Ignoring her impudent glance, he passed his fingers carefully over the column of her throat. 'Is that tender?'

'Course . . . got a punch on it, didn't I? Copped the one that was meant for my feller. We had a fight, see, down on the quay, right set-to it was.' She unwrapped a strip of chewing gum and chewed on it happily. She had a broken front tooth—a right incisor. 'Oh, that was done different,' she said, 'ran into a door, didn't I?' She closed one eye in a wink. 'Next time it'll be my flippin' nose!'

Ian saw his other three patients, then conferred with Kate in her office. 'That's two off your hands.' He had just that moment told Mrs Fawley that the little girl, Emily, could be discharged next day. 'That just leaves Miss Clifford, the mastoid, and Mrs Tremaine, of course. I'm operating on Mrs Tremaine tomorrow morning at ten. And yes, I have informed theatre staff, so no need for you to bother. Miss Clifford should be fit for discharge on Thursday of next week. I expect Miss Rone has told you that I can admit up to four patients in each of Penhallow and Fratton Wards over the next few months?'

'She has, yes. Oh, thank you, Zia,' said Kate, as the

ward domestic tapped at the door and came in with a tray of tea. There were two cups and a plate of shortbreads; she looked across at Ian. He had refused tea yesterday, would today be different? It seemed that it was.

'That looks just the job,' he commented.

Kate remembered how he liked his tea—a little milk and no sugar, and he loved biscuits; he thanked her and took two. 'When the child goes out tomorrow,' he said, in between healthy bites, 'will you be moving Mrs Proudman into the big ward again?'

'I think so, yes,' said Kate, 'for the remainder of her stay. I expect Mr Jarman will let her go home once her stitches are out.'

'So could you put Anne Tremaine with Miss Clifford?'

'Of course, if that's what you want—leaving one of the side-wards free, you mean?'

'That's exactly what I mean. It's for a patient suffering from bone disease, causing intractable pain. She's been passed to me by Briggs Hughes, and we both of us consider she could be greatly helped by excising her pituitary gland.'

'I see, yes.'

'She's a Mrs Bealer. I would like to admit her on Monday. I intend to do a hypophysectomy, using the nasal route. She's not a very *easy* woman . . . she wouldn't mix well in the ward.'

'That's all right, I'll keep the side-ward free,' Kate got up and made a note, 'unless, of course,' she sat down again, 'Mr Jarman instructs me otherwise. I can't see that happening, though.'

'No, neither can I. I know Bill Jarman, he and I have worked together before. He's not the sort to make difficulties, just for the sake of it.

'He's a very nice man,' commented Kate.

'Yes, he is.'

'Pleasant and easy to deal with.' Their conversation was petering out, but Kate tried to keep it going. She tried to think of things to say, for any silence between them wouldn't be easy, and might lead to danger-spots. Ian wasn't looking at her, he was staring down at his cup. It was then that she knew without any doubt that his mind was forming questions. He was going to ask her about her sister and Hugh.

'I haven't asked about Rose and the Prof. How are they getting on? Any family yet?' His voice was low, his glance mildly enquiring; he was making it easy. Kate hastened to reply.

'They're well, thank you,' she smiled at him. 'Rose is expecting a baby . . . their first, towards the end of August.'

'I take it that's good news?'

'The best, yes . . . they're both very thrilled.'

He nodded, holding her eyes. 'Tell me about yourself, Kate. Has Daniel been moved down here? I seem to remember him saying he wished his firm would transfer him.' Daniel Browning had been an architect with Fitzjohns & Rawlings, an expanding firm, with branches all over the south.

Kate stared at Ian; she kept on staring, she couldn't look away. His face seemed to go a long way off, then move in close again. He didn't know about Danny, he didn't know he had died. Well, of course he didn't, because who would have told him? He had been out of touch for so long. So tell him then, just tell him, get it over with . . . just tell him; but she couldn't frame the words.

'What's up? What's wrong? Have I been tactless? Have you and Daniel parted?' His eyes, blue as a summer sea, showed concern and curiosity. Kate thought they held derision too, she felt sure he was thinking, she's following in her mother's footsteps . . . another broken marriage. Her family aren't all that strong on staying power. He might have been thinking of the split with Rose too, he almost certainly was.

'Danny died,' she cried in a burst of outrage. 'He died nearly two years ago! He died after months of illness . . . trying to get well. I nursed him, I got compassionate leave.'

She heard the low exclamation he gave, she saw him through a blur, heard his cup hit the saucer, then saw him come round the desk. His white coat filled her vision, and she felt the weight of his arm about her shoulders; she heard his muttered: 'Kate . . . what *can* I say?'

'Nothing . . . it's all right, you weren't to know.' She stared at the end of the desk. The nearness of him, the way he spoke, nearly broke her up. She wanted to turn, to lean against him, to have him hold her tightly. She wanted to lay her head on his front and bawl like a baby. Instead she stiffened, and the comforting arm fell away.

'Like to tell me about it?' He sat on the desk, getting a foreshortened view of her nose and brow, and wings of light-brown hair.

'No, not really. Thank you, though. I would like to get back on the ward. You stay here and finish your tea.' She could not look at him. Somehow or other she got to her feet, left the room and shut the door. She found she was trembling, she felt she could hardly breathe.

Through the large square viewing window Ian watched her walk down the ward—straight-backed, head high, legs long and slender, moving beneath the hem of her navy dress. He wondered where she was living and why she had come to Cornwall. He remembered Daniel Browning as a flamboyant, showing-off type. He had thought them ill-matched, which was partly why he had made that gaffe just now. Opposites attracted and very often settled down well together. What a crass idiot to say what I did . . . why didn't I keep my mouth shut? he thought angrily. Leaving the office, he went over to Fratton Ward.

As Kate garaged the Fiat at the side of the cottage some two hours later, she saw Ellis Rand on the other side of the hedge.

'May I come over, Mrs Browning?' He was in khaki shorts and T-shirt; he had been gardening, she could smell the newly-cut grass.

'Of course, please do.' Her heart sank a little, for she wanted nothing more than to shower and change, then sit down in the cool.

He pushed through the hedge, holding the fronds well away from his shoulders, and joined her on the brick path, hair a little untidy, face hot and darkened by the sun. 'It's been a scorcher, hasn't it . . . too hot to work?'

'Yes, very hot.' Kate looked at his hand. 'Has your finger been troubling you?'

'Oh, no, nothing like that. I'm not in bother this time. Actually, I wondered,' he thrust his hands in the pockets of his shorts, 'if you would like to stroll down the hill and have a drink at the Smugglers' Arms. It needn't take long, if you don't want it to, but I would like to say some kind of "thank you" for the good turn you did me yesterday.'

'Mr Rand, it was nothing,' she protested.

'To me it meant a very great deal,' he said. 'I was able to work to get over the misery of a chapter that wouldn't come right. I finished it at lunchtime, did some gardening, now I want to relax.' His hands came out of his pockets and he laced them behind his back. Somehow or other Ellis Rand never knew what to do with his hands; when not in use they frequently hampered him. 'Of course,' he went on, giving her a loophole, 'you may feel too tired to come out.'

'Not at all,' she smiled at him, 'I think it's a great idea.' And she meant it too, for she suddenly thought what a change it would be to go out. What a change it would be to talk with someone who wasn't 'hospital'. 'Give me ten minutes to freshen up,' she said, getting out her key.

'Me too.' Ellis backed down the path, making for the gate. 'I don't usually go out looking like a cross-country runner . . . bad for my image. What would my readers say?'

So, she thought, he can laugh at himself, he's really rather nice. As for me, I don't go out enough, I spend all my off-time at home. That's not very sensible, not very balanced, especially for a nurse. I don't want any male entanglements—at least, not the heavy kind, but all the same I mustn't turn into a dreary workaholic because that, Kate Browning, is the road to loneliness.

Upstairs in the hot little bedroom directly under the roof, she stepped into a cotton dress with a circular patterned skirt. She brushed her hair loose and discarded her tights, then buckled on soft leather sandals. Her face with its pointed chin and high cheekbones was already lightly tanned, a dusting of freckles ran across her nose.

It was pleasant walking down the hill in the company of Ellis Rand, pleasant to sit on the paved forecourt of the timbered public house that had once been a famous coaching inn. He told her a little about his writing, and how he felt about it. 'In a sense it's even more worrying when you've had one success,' he said. 'Success creates a pressure, one has a standard to keep up. And you're on your own with it, solitary, which leaves room for creeping doubts. Some days I would give the earth to have someone of my own kind, someone who could be objective, to talk my plots over with. Keeping one's confidence on the ascendant, keeping one's judgments right, isn't easy . . . one needs a sounding-board.'

'I think I know what you mean,' said Kate, hoping she did. It was very difficult for someone like her, who worked within a team, to imagine going solo. It wouldn't suit me, she thought. I like the framework of a team, I like the team spirit, the running-in-harness, the feeling of comradeship. 'But still,' she went on, hoping to take the harassed look from his face, 'there are many advantages, aren't there, in your kind of work—one of them being that it's moveable, you can spend your summers down here, or anywhere else that suits you, or suits the book, of course.'

'True,' he said, but now it was he who sounded unconvincing. They watched a kittiwake coming in to land, practically over their heads, they could see its legs hanging straight and strong, its wide span of wing, then its yellow beak as it perched on the mast of a boat.

'Cornwall is like a bright jewel the summer,' Kate said dreamily, 'and this north-west coast is the best part of all, I'd like to live here for ever.'

'For ever is a very long time,' said Ellis, a little prosaically.

'Yes, maybe.' Her eyes were still dreamy, looking out to sea.

'Are you a widow?'

'Yes,' she replied, 'my husband died last year.' And how strange it was that she found it so easy to tell Ellis Rand this, whereas telling Ian had left her emotionally torn. He was silent for some minutes, and to get him talking again she asked him if he knew when his book would be televised. 'Have you got the exact dates? Do you know when we shall see it?'

'It's to run in twelve weekly parts, starting the eighth

of November,' he told her. 'The central character, Bill Stretham, the detective, is to be played by John Christy. I met him just before I came down here, and he fits the part exactly. He's Bill Stretham to the last eyelash. I couldn't be more pleased.'

'I'm glad to hear it.'

He looked at her sharply. Was she sending him up? Colour swept into his face, his eyes looked angry and hard. 'If I'm boring you, say so, but as you asked . . .'

'Oh, Ellis, I'm sorry,' she cried, 'of course you're not boring me . . . nothing like. I'm just marvelling at the way things turn out. John Christy is my father!' She carolled the words, and pride rang in her voice.

He looked disbelieving. '*What?*' he exclaimed.

'John Christy is my father.'

'Good heavens! I . . . can't believe it!'

'Nevertheless, it's true.'

'But I've met his wife, and she looked so young!'

'She's not my mother, Ellis. My parents divorced, and Pa married again, ten years ago. Maxine, his wife, is in her thirties. They have two little boys . . . my half-brothers, ages seven and five.'

'Good heavens!' he repeated. It seemed to be all he could say.

'I see them when I can,' Kate told him, 'although not so often now. At home it was easy, as they live in Kensington.'

'I know they do—I went to their house.' Ellis pushed back his chair. 'But what an amazing coincidence that we should meet up like this!'

'I agree . . . yes. And as neighbours too.'

'And I nearly didn't come. I saw the cottage advertised, but was told it was fully booked. I only got it in the end because of a cancellation. There's little doubt about it, real life is stranger than fiction.' One of his rather shy smiles broadened out his face. His teeth were square with an overlap in front. 'Does your father know you're in Cornwall?' he asked.

'Oh yes, we keep in touch. He and Maxine and the children are coming here in August, just for a break. They're staying at Newquay, at the Talland Head Hotel. When Pa comes to the cottage, as he's bound to, you must come in and meet him again. He's crazy about this part of the world. We think alike on that.'

'You resemble him in appearance, you have his eyes and brow.' Kate's eyes were green hazel and widely set, her brow was the rounded kind that looked untroubled even when it was not. She was amused at Ellis's perusal of her features, for that was what he was doing—perusing her, like checking a page of his book. I doubt if he knew what I looked like before, she thought with a touch of pique. 'Is his wife an actress?' he asked. He was back to her father; she gave a little shrug.

'She was, but not now. She gave up when she married, gave her all to coping with Pa. He's not the easiest man in the world to live beside, you know. The artistic temperament needs skilful handling, and a mountain of tolerance.'

'I'm with you there, every inch of the way.' Ellis sounded, for him, quite fierce. Perhaps he had lived with a girl who hadn't appreciated his talent. Perhaps the liaison hadn't worked well, had made him miserable. Yet for all his air of 'don't-come-too-close', Kate felt he looked like a man who would settle down well into marriage with the right kind of girl. She would have to be fairly placid and tough, yet understand his writing, and its rigours, and what it did to her man. Yes, Ellis needed praise and reassurance. He needed feeding too. Men on their own very often took to eating out of packets. Should she ask him to supper? she wondered, as they walked back up the hill. She toyed with the idea for several minutes, then decided not to suggest it. He would only refuse and say he wanted to work.

He told her about his parents, who were teachers in the North. 'They both work, always have done. I was a latch-key kid.'

'No brothers or sisters?'

'No, just me.'

'I have a sister,' she said. 'There's a year between us, I'm the younger, and we came close when our parents divorced. I married young, at eighteen, which made a difference, of course. Now Rose is married, and I'm not, which again makes a difference.'

'Marriage is something I haven't tried,' Ellis said in a muffled voice, kicking a round pebble into the kerb.

'It doesn't suit everyone.'

The faint smile he gave baffled her a little, and kept her quiet till they reached their respective gates. 'I'm glad we're neighbours,' he said, as they prepared to part company. 'But the fact of your being *who* you are still amazes me.'

'John Christy being my father, you mean?' She could see that added glamour made her more interesting in his eyes, which was understandable. He might even, she thought, ask me out now and then, and if he does, I'll go. She liked him, he was unusual; she was glad he had met her father. It made the fact of him living next door for the rest of the summer seem part of a pattern, as though it had been meant.

CHAPTER THREE

MRS PROUDMAN'S stitches were removed on Tuesday, and when William Jarman saw her, he pronounced her fit enough to be discharged. 'Don's thrilled about it,' she told Kate, after visiting time was done. 'He's not managed very well without me, he's not domesticated. My daughter would have helped him out, but she lives in Aberdeen. Her husband is on one of the oil rigs, and Fay's got a job of her own. You can't expect people to upset their own lives, not for two short weeks.'

'That's true enough.' Kate moved to close the windows in the day room. A monsoon-like rain was bashing down outside.

'But apart from worrying about my Don, I've enjoyed my stay in here. I shall miss all those gorgeous doctors,' Mrs Proudman heaved a sigh. 'Since I've been back in the big ward, though, I've not seen that fair-haired one—the one who looks like a Norseman and carries himself like a god.'

'My goodness, he's made an impression!' Kate looked at her and laughed. 'You mean Mr Casson, and you're making him sound like the hero in your book!' The paperback novel lying face upwards on Mrs Proudman's lap showed a proud Viking stepping out from his boat.

'Yes, I know, I fantasise. I think most women do.' Mrs Proudman brought her thoughts back to her rotund little husband and his stubby warmth, and she sighed with pleasure again.

'Mr Casson comes in the afternoons, usually. He fits in with Mr Jarman. He's only here for a few months while the ENT Hospital is being repaired. He's not one of our regular staff.' Kate hadn't seen him since Friday, and then she had only just glimpsed him in his theatre greens and concealing mask, when she had taken Anne Tremaine to theatre block for surgery on her nose.

'Talk of the devil, he's here now!' Mrs Proudman hissed. 'I can see him through in the corridor with the nurse who wears a white dress.'

He was talking to Pat Finn, the agency nurse, Kate saw as she turned round. Nurse Finn, who was proving to be a great help on both the surgical wards, was standing there with a pile of sheets, listening to Ian Casson expounding on . . . what, for goodness' sake? It sounded like photography. Kate caught the words, 'lens' and 'shade' and 'light meter', as she got within hearing distance. 'Nurse Finn and I both belong to the local Camera Club, Sister,' Ian explained, smiling over at her. Pat Finn, elfin and dark, with a fringe that touched her brows, excused herself, and went into the ward with her sheets.

'Is photography one of your hobbies, sir?' Kate showed him into the office.

'Yes, it is . . . recently acquired. I find it fascinating.' There was a dark smattering of rain on the shoulders of his suit—a light grey suit with a blue and navy tie. He closed the door and reached for his coat, which hung on the back of it. 'How's Mrs Bealer settling in?' The starched white coat was stiff, and newly laundered; he left the buttons undone.

'Restless, which is understandable.' She handed him the notes. 'Your houseman saw her yesterday, and arranged for several tests. You'll find the lab reports are all in there.'

'I see them, thank you.' He studied the findings. 'All right, let's go in and see her.' Moving swiftly, he opened

the door with a little swish and flourish. Kate could feel
his eyes on her as she brushed past him, then heard him
greet Staff Nurse True, who was coming out of the sluice
with a tray of jars.

Mrs Bealer had been an in-patient for just on twenty-
four hours. She was anxious to have the operation,
which she knew would relieve her pain, but she hated
waiting, and she hated hospitals. She was middle-aged,
parchment-skinned, with a handsome, haggard face; she
had grey hair held back with a slide. When she saw Ian
and Kate come in she jerked away from her pillows. Ian
smiled and gently eased her back. 'Well, it's good to see
you again, Mrs Bealer.' (He had been seeing her in
Outpatients with Mr Briggs-Hughes during the last few
weeks). 'Now we'll be able to do something for you, get
rid of that tiresome pain.'

'Yes, but *when*?' Janet Bealer fixed tired eyes on his
face. 'If you're going to operate I want it done soon, I
can't stand this waiting about.'

'Before I operate there are one or two tests I need to
carry out. They're routine for this type of surgery, and
very necessary.'

'I get bored, and worked up too,' she sighed.

'That's understandable. Perhaps your husband could
bring you in some knitting, or sewing—something like
that to keep you occupied.'

Mrs Bealer and Kate exchanged glances of amused
exasperation. There were times when men, even clever
ones . . . especially clever ones, had few clues about
what made women tick. Not all women were needlework addicts; Janet Bealer wasn't. Kate knew this, for
the day before the two of them had talked. Each had
discovered that the other had little enthusiasm for mend-
ing, or sewing, or knitting cardigans. So they smiled at
one another now, and a little bond was formed. It was

then that Kate became what Janet Bealer would later describe as: 'my ally and friend, who never let me down.'

Back in the office Ian gave further treatment instructions to Kate: 'Continue her analgesia, of course, right up to surgery. Start the penicillin now, 1 mega-unit six-hourly. We'll begin cortisone therapy the day after tomorrow. I'd like another blood count and another two films of her chest. It seemed to me to be hot in her room, too hot for her anyway,' he added. 'Perhaps you could fix her up with a fan, a small one to stand on her locker. I plan to operate in a week or ten days, if all her tests are okay. I know you'll do all you can to help her over this period.'

'I intend to spend part of each day,' Kate affirmed, 'simply keeping her company. I can see she needs special care.'

'You're a caring person, aren't you?' He turned and met her eyes, and something in his voice and expression —an underlying softness, a kind of sweetness—made her throat constrict. It put her on her guard too. I will not let him get to me, I will not let him undermine my resolves, I will not come under his spell . . .

'I care about my patients, yes,' she smiled, but her words had an edge. His eyes left hers.

'I assumed that's what we were talking about,' he said. He moved from the desk to the window, and stared out at the rain. She saw his hands open and close, then he was turning round, picking up two sets of folders, opening the one on top. 'As I'm in rather a rush, perhaps we could see Anne Tremaine and the Clifford girl,' he tapped the former's notes. 'I see her cavity has drained well, which in all probability means that it will heal up without further help from me. All right then, Sister, ready when you are.' He let Kate reach the door first, then followed her out, jaw hard, blue eyes shuttered, mouth getting ready to smile at Anne Tremaine.

After he had seen both patients and gone back to the Clinic, Kate started on her paperwork, but couldn't concentrate. He's charming and he knows it, he's fully aware of his powers, she thought. He's what might be termed a practised operator, in more ways than one. She tried to laugh, but failed to do so; she didn't feel amused. And I'm not even an especially susceptible female, she thought, as she went off duty. Danny was the only man I ever loved.

As she drove past the Cathedral she decided to go to the shops and try to buy a copy of Ellis's book. She very much wanted to read it, she would ask him to autograph it. How very different he was from Ian . . . with Ellis she could relax and feel at ease, instead of on tenterhooks.

Smiths hadn't got *Bland Justice*. 'We've sold out,' the assistant said, 'but there are more on order, they should be in next month.' Next month was too long a time to wait; Kate decided to go to Grants on the other side of the city, out of the central zone. Here she was lucky, there was one copy left. Persistence wins in the end, she told herself, as she left the shop with the book.

She was about to get back into the Fiat when she realised where she was—only two streets from Tolcanbury Hill and the Royal ENT Clinic. She might as well see what it looked like, see how the work was going. She found it easily, and drew up outside its gates. It looked horrendous even now, even after a week. The eastern wing, which she rightly assumed to be the Outpatients' Block, was shored up and encased in scaffolding. Tarpaulins hung from the scaffolding, workmen's vans and lorries made a sorry mess of the yard surround— cement-mixers and sand-heaps, bricks and timber, stuck out from plastic sheets. The rain had ceased with suddenness, as summer rain often does, but lakes and pools of water remained, milky with lime and chalk; tin-hatted workmen were slopping through to their vans.

Kate thought she had better get out of their way, and it was then that she saw Ian waving to her from the other side of the road. Of course, he lived opposite . . . she hadn't forgotten, but hadn't thought he would be in. He was making come-on beckoning movements, like a traffic controller, guiding and waving her into his drive. It wasn't so much a drive as a side-way, as his house was one of a terrace—an attractive Georgian terrace called Tolcanbury Close. It didn't occur to her not to obey the summons of that arm. She pulled up in the side-way, and rolled the window down. 'Many thanks, you saved me getting tangled up with that lot,' she indicated the convoy of lorries and vans.

'That's what I thought.' He peered under the roof. 'What brings you out this way?'

She told him the reason quickly, not wanting him to think she had made the detour on the chance of seeing him. 'Someone I know has written a book, and I wanted to buy it,' she said. 'I couldn't get it in Bridge Street, so thought I'd try at Grants.'

'The shops out of the city centre have their uses, I find.' He could see the book on the seat beside her —*Bland Justice* by Ellis Rand. He had read it himself and thought it excellent. How had she got to know Rand? he wondered . . . in London, most likely . . . probably through her father at one of his many parties. John Christy was one of the outgoing kind. 'Come in and see my consulting rooms,' he gestured back at the house, 'I took them over with the rest of the place from Carlton, my predecessor. I've had alterations made to suit me, I'd like to show you over.' His fingers curled in the handle of her door.

She hesitated, making no move at all to undo her

safety-belt. Ian grinned at her through the open window, his eyes glinting amusement. 'Come, Kate, we're not quite strangers, are we, and my housekeeper's on the premises! Of course,' his expression sobered a little, 'you may have something else on.'

'No, I haven't, not until later.' She got out of the car and followed him up the steps of the house, not missing his name: IAN CASSON, FRCS on the iron railings outside.

His rooms were well equipped and planned, they opened out from the hall—a waiting-room and office on the left-hand side, a consulting room on the right. At the back, and down a short stretch of passage, was a dining-room and kitchen. The kitchen was huge, and in it Mrs MacTavish, Ian's housekeeper, looked even smaller than the five-foot-two she was. Her hair was grizzled, she was shelling peas, but she stopped to shake hands with Kate. 'Ye look awfu' young to be a Sister.'

'They get younger every day, just like the policemen,' Ian said with a laugh. 'Mrs Mac comes from midday until eight o'clock each night,' he explained to Kate as they left the kitchen and walked up the passage again. 'The hours suit her, and they suit me, I lunch at the Clinic usually, have my evening meal here after my patients have gone. I have three coming this evening, and no nurse/secretary. She's gone home with a streaming cold; I've prescribed hot lemon and bed.'

'Oh dear, poor woman, but how awkward for you.' Kate made all the right noises.

'I shall manage, I expect.'

'What time are they coming—your private patients, I mean?'

'Between five-thirty and seven-thirty.' She saw him look at his watch. They had nearly reached the front door with its fanlight and insets of glass. 'Miss Latham is invaluable with my young child patients. Mothers, as you know, aren't *always* the best people to calm their fears.'

'That's true.' There was silence. Neither spoke for one long ticking moment, then: 'Have you any children coming this evening?' asked Kate, clearing her throat.

'I have . . . two, and after them a blind man for ear syringing—a tricky programme.' He reached to open the door.

'I could help you, if you'd like me to.' She had no sooner made the offer than she realised he had meant her to do just that. She could see it in his beaming glance, and she stared straight back at him, letting him see she knew what he was about.

'That's very good of you . . . most kind.' He had the grace to flush. And now it was Kate's turn to look away, for she didn't want him to see she was flattered by his wily manoeuvrings. He wanted her help, and weakly she acknowledged how very much that pleased her. It's called falling into a trap on purpose, she thought, going into the office, and listening while he explained where everything was.

The role of nurse-receptionist-secretary was a new one for Kate, but she had to admit she enjoyed the experience—answering the front door bell, showing the patient—each child accompanied by an adult—into the big low-windowed consulting room. She held one nervous little girl on her lap, while Ian examined her throat. The next, a boy who was with his father, refused to open his mouth until he had finished a large piece of toffee that stretched his face to grotesqueness and clung round his teeth like so much glutinous paste. 'I shouldn't have let him have it, should I?' the father said helplessly, as they all sat watching the small boy chew.

The last, and third patient, the blind man, arrived in a

taxicab. The driver helped him out and up the steps. He left his long white cane in the office, while Kate took him through to Ian, who syringed his right ear, cleaning out debris and wax. 'I'm used to not seeing,' he told Kate, as she untied his plastic bib, 'but hearing means everything to me, it makes up for so much. I'm musical, I play a bit—the piano, you know. And next month I'm going to London for the Proms.'

'I love the Promenade Concerts, but I shall miss them this year,' said Kate, cautioning Mr Kelter to sit still for a few minutes, in case he should be dizzy, just at first. Ian chatted to him then, and on looking at his notes, Kate saw that he was sixty-seven and has lost his sight in the war, at Dunkirk, forty-six years ago. He had been blind since he was twenty-one, not much more than a boy. She watched Ian lead him through to the passage outside.

'He teaches Braille at the School for Blind Children just outside Pelruth,' he told Kate, when he came back from helping Mr Kelter into the taxi which Kate had summoned by phone. 'He lives with his unmarried sister; his wife left him years ago, went off with an American . . . that's womankind for you!'

'We're not all made in the same mould, don't lump us all together!' retorted Kate, as Mrs MacTavish came in.

'Excuse me, sir, but will the young leddy be staying on to supper? It's a duck . . . a faine bird, plenty for two.'

Ian looked at Kate, who shook her head. 'It sounds tempting, but I can't. I've got my neighbour coming in for a meal.' And this was no excuse. It was perfectly true, for since last Thursday Ellis had changed his attitude. He appeared to regard her as a friend now, seeming to have lost his fear that she might be a nuisance and stop him trying to work. She was on the point of telling Ian who her neighbour was, then decided not to, since Ellis might want his whereabouts kept a secret, just for the summer; Pinnocks might be a retreat.

'I wish you'd told me you were having a guest.' Ian sounded troubled. 'I must have run you right up against time. You should have mentioned it, Kate.'

'We're not eating till nine, so it doesn't matter.' Her eyes strayed to the clock, whose hands indicated seven-fifteen.

'Would you like some strawberries to take home with you? There's a surfeit in the garden. If you don't have them Mrs Mac will be feeding them to me for weeks, which means I'll most likely come out in a strawberry rash!'

'Well, thank you, I'd love some.' Strawberries and cream would make an alternative pudding to the nectarines at home, which might not be properly ripe.

'I'll help you pick them, I'll get a basket.' Ian turned towards the kitchen. 'Come out this way, it leads to the vegetable patch.'

For a town garden the vegetable patch was large, and square, and prolific. It looked as though it grew everything, from cabbages to spinach, from currants to strawberries, from grapes to peaches—the latter in a greenhouse; there was even a fig tree in a corner by itself. The sun, which had come out after the rain, was already drying the soil. They could feel it on the backs of their hands, as they stretched them over the strawberry bed, freeing the luscious fruit from its welter of leaves. Looking at Ian with his jacket off, wrists sticking out from his cuffs, long surgeon's fingers employed on their menial task, Kate was reminded of earlier times, of the times when she and Danny used to make up a four with him and Rose. Did he think of Rose very often now? Had he got several girl-friends, or was he in love with Helen Reever—pretty, curvaceous and rich . . . and potty about him; that much was obvious.

'Ian, this is far more than I'll need.' She turned and went back to the path.

'Sure?' He stood up, wiping his hands on a cotton handkerchief.

'Absolutely.'

'Okay, then.' He began to walk towards her, lifting his legs carefully over the rows. She watched him coming, the sun on his hair, blazing it to gold, turning his shirt to stark white, shadowing his eyes. As he reached her he smiled, and as she smiled back she felt a kind of joining, a thrust of feeling, not flashing, not swift, but slow and strong and compelling. She couldn't have moved, she stood there on the path. She knew what would happen. Ian set down the basket, straightened and drew her towards him, cupping her shoulders, bringing her close, wrapping his arms round her back to bring her closer, resting his face on her hair. A feeling of well-being coursed through her, warming her blood like wine. The comfort of holding, of being held, the fit of body on body, was a mulling delight, a heavy pleasure that lightened, then quickened and flared to a blazing joy as he brought his mouth to hers.

How long the kiss lasted she had no idea. She heard him murmur her name; it sang in her ears, and it posed a question, and somehow she freed herself. 'No, Ian, no! I'm sorry . . . no!' She turned and fled from him. She reached the drive, she could see the top of her car.

He had followed her, he was close behind. 'There's no need to run from me, Kate. You've forgotten your strawberries.' He gave them to her and she took them with shaking hands. 'And your handbag and book are still inside my house.'

'I'll go and get them.' She tried to push past him, but he effectively blocked her way.

'Wait here, I'll get them . . . just *wait*, will you?' He

was giving her orders again. And somehow that helped; she nodded and watched him go.

The embrace shouldn't have happened, it shouldn't, *shouldn't* have happened. He would want to bring it to its logical conclusion, and in no way did Kate intend to have an affair . . . not just for fun, and certainly not with him. She wouldn't be good at a temporary involvement, and aside from anything else, Ian had once been engaged to her sister Rose, which made the whole thing farcical, like a TV sit-com. She choked back hysterical mirth.

Ian collected her handbag and paperback, then came back down the steps. She was standing tall and straight and rigid in front of her yellow car. 'Save your speeches,' he said, when he reached her. 'I know what you're going to say.'

Kate met his eyes—it was easier now, being apart had helped, and nothing was ever solved by evasion. She felt a surge of relief. 'It's just that I don't want to complicate things. I like my life as it is.'

'I like mine too.' He was laughing, the amused note was back in his voice, his smile was wide, but his eyes were expressionless.

'I don't want any follow-ups.' A little kick of anger at his attitude of reasonableness made her choke out the words.

'Then we won't have them . . . simple . . . or no problem, as they say. I don't force myself on people, Kate. I'm lucky enough not to have to. So let's shake on it, shall we, no follow-ups?' As she reached for the car door, he caught at her hand and pumped it up and down.

And now she was angry, and so was he. Hers showed, his was concealed. 'Thank you for your help with my patients.' He watched her slam the door and start to reverse, as he guided her out of his drive.

I behaved like a clot, she reflected, trying to cool down as she drove home . . . what a fuss to make over a kiss! I asked for it too, I stood there on the path and let it happen. I kissed him back with all that was in me, then fled and told him off. Still, he didn't care, he had shown her that . . . plenty more fish in the sea, had been written all over his arrogant face. Kate wished Ellis wasn't coming to supper. She didn't feel like company, but she couldn't put him off at this late hour. She timed the meal for nine o'clock, making a green salad and putting two porterhouse steaks out ready to grill. She tipped the strawberries out of the basket and washed them at the sink, nipping the stalks out and feeling . . . *dreadful* . . . all over again. It was then that she realised with a terrible jolt just how much Ian attracted her . . . she admitted it to herself and was appalled.

Ellis arrived exactly on time, spruce in a new pair of jeans, cream ones, with a dark green sweater on top. He had bought a bottle of rosé wine to go with the steaks, and commented on how fresh the strawberries looked. 'They were picked this evening from a . . . a friend's garden,' said Kate in a strangled voice. Ellis was straining to uncork the wine, so missed the look on her face; he was hungry and looking forward to his meal.

They ate in the sitting-room-cum-dining-room, beyond the windows of which the cupressus hedge which divided the gardens loomed black as twilight came. From where they sat they could see the lights down in the little harbour, see them twinkling on in groups round the curved bay, threading like a necklace up the hill. Kate switched on the centre ceiling lamp, flooding the room with glare. She was glad to see Ellis doing justice to the meal.

'You must let me take you out one evening, as a small return,' he said. He had cheese and crackers after the strawberries, fondants with coffee. 'I've made a pig of myself, I know, but I forget about food when I'm writing, then when I start to eat I never stop.'

'You don't have to mind about that, Ellis. I'm only too glad you enjoyed it. And you don't have to repay me, either, I like you being here.' As she said this she knew she meant it; he might be a little withdrawn, a reserved man, even secretive, but this didn't trouble her. She knew that for quite a lot of the time he had to sink into thought, everything had to be secondary to his work.

They left the washing-up and adjourned to the sitting end of the room. It was then that Ellis asked her, with a good deal of diffidence, if she could give him her views, as a woman, on a scene in his manuscript. 'I need to talk it over with someone . . . I need an outside viewpoint.'

'Try me!' Kate drew the curtains. It's my evening for helping, she thought, feeling a little stab in her breast as she brought to mind Ian's patients—the oneness and closeness she had felt with him, as they dealt with the two children, and the elderly man blinded at Dunkirk.

But as Ellis unfolded part of his plot, as they discussed it together, as she gave him her views, for what they were worth, the earlier part of the evening shunted backwards, and Kate became as enthusiastic as he was. And how lucky he was, how very lucky to be so talented. Ellis could always escape from reality, shut the real world out. He could dwell in the one he chose to create out of his imaginings. He could live in his own land of make-believe.

CHAPTER FOUR

KATE was spared having to meet Ian next day, for his Registrar, Annika Weiss, a buxom blonde of Swiss descent, came to the ward with his houseman, two young medical students at their heels. They spent most of their time with Mrs Bealer, and her case was explained to the students; Kate could see her getting more and more annoyed.

'What do they think I am—a stuffed dummy!' she exploded when they had gone.

'The students have to learn, Mrs Bealer.'

'Not on me they don't!'

'I understand how you felt, and I'm sorry.' Kate gave her hand a squeeze.

'I may not have the operation, they can't make me have it—I shall please myself, I know my rights, I may decide to go home. And it's no good you saying anything, Sister.' Mrs Bealer vented her anger on Kate. 'You're on their side when it comes to it, I can see it on your face.'

'Mrs Bealer, we're all on the same side, *your* side. We want you to get well.' Kate longed to say more, but had the nous not to labour the point. Instead she pulled up a chair and sat down, and listened silently while Janet Bealer finished her long tirade.

She calmed down at last, Kate made her some tea, and gave her two of her tablets. And she found herself hoping, after all, that Ian would come next day. He had a way with Janet—yes, he even got through to *her*. That charm of his could work in diverse ways.

56

The following day, Thursday, just after visiting time, Helen Reever came to the ward with a sheaf of pink carnations. She found Kate in her office, and called out from the doorway: 'I always came straight up to the ward when Sister Stubbs was here, so I hope you don't mind.' Then, as Kate turned round, they recognised one another; Helen spoke first, advancing into the room. 'We've met, haven't we, here at the hospital, in the yard the other day? I didn't realise you were on Penhallow, but I'm very glad you are.'

Why, Kate wondered, why should she be glad? She took the sheaf of flowers. 'I'm Kate Browning, the new Sister,' she said.

'I'm Helen Reever, the florist . . . sounds like Happy Families, doesn't it!' The two young women shook hands.

'I see these are for Mrs Vane.' Kate looked at the card on the flowers. 'You can take them in to her, if you like.'

'Oh no, I'll leave that to you. I only deliver them hand-to-hand if I actually know the patient. Even then it depends on the Sister, there are still some battleaxe ones.'

'I know,' Kate laughed, and so did Helen Reever. She looked older this afternoon, still brightly but very sharply turned out in a yellow linen skirt and a shirt-blouse open at the neck. Why, she's probably as old as I am, Kate thought. How different she seems today! She looks every bit the keen businesswoman that Olly said she was. Nevertheless, I wish she would go, I've no time to stand and talk. 'Is there anything else, Miss Reever? Were you wanting something else?' she asked pleasantly, moving towards her desk.

'Oh, call me Helen.' She sat when Kate did, much to the latter's dismay. 'I won't keep you long, I can see you're busy, but I just wanted to mention . . . to tell you about a patient who's coming in next week . . . here into Penhallow Ward, I mean.'

'I see.' Kate stiffened. Surely Helen knew she couldn't discuss a patient. Hadn't she heard of hospital ethics and rules?

'It's my old nanny, my old nurse,' Helen went on, undeterred. 'She's due to come in next Tuesday. She's got a hiatus hernia, and Willie Jarman's operating. Her name's Adela Norton and she's seventy-four—I expect you know about her.' Kate did, for as it happened Miss Norton's medical file, sent up from Outpatients, was amongst the pile on her desk. 'She's a poppet, you'll love her,' Helen rattled on, 'she brought me up from a baby—we lived at Camborne then. She was Mother's nurse too, so she's really what you might call a family retainer; she was very upset when my parents went abroad. I think she thought I would go too, but I didn't, I stayed in England and trained as a florist with Sholter-fords in London . . . one can't go better than that. Then Daddy bought me my business here, with a flat over the top. Norty lives out at Poldenack, so I see her most days. Well, anyway,' she gave a small laugh, 'what I'm trying to ask you is . . . will you keep an eye on her, see that she's all right? I wanted her to go privately, but she wasn't having that. I'd have paid and seen to everything for her.'

'She'll have very good treatment here. Mr Jarman's a wonderful surgeon, and as to the nursing part, she'll have every care and attention, all our patients . . .' A tap on the door interrupted Kate; it opened and Ian came in. He nodded formally in Kate's direction, then saw Helen and smiled.

'Hello, Nell . . . what brings you here?'

'Floral tributes, what else!' Helen rose from her chair and looked up at him. She was small to his six foot one, at least a head and neck shorter . . . as high as his heart, Kate thought. Other thoughts rippled in after that, and all of them were painful. Why didn't she go? Why didn't she move? The ward is my domain . . . why doesn't she go, and leave us to our work?

'I shan't be all that long today.' Ian was turning round and walking with Helen into the corridor. There was a mutter of 'tea' and 'main entrance' and 'don't you dare stand me up', and then he was coming back in and looking amused and pleased with himself.

'Everything all right? No alarms or excursions?' His enquiring gaze met Kate's. There was nothing in his eyes to embarrass her, they looked much as they always did whenever he came sauntering on to the ward. So she told him, looking as impassive as he, that Miss Clifford had gone home that morning; that Anne Tremaine wanted to see him about her own discharge; and that Mrs Bealer was bored and down in the dumps. They were just about to visit Mrs Bealer when Kate's telephone rang. Ian slid the file of notes from her hand. 'All right, you deal with that . . . one of your nurses can chaperon me,' and before she could say a word, he accosted Pat Finn who had come in for Mrs Vane's sheaf of flowers. 'Leave those, Nurse, and come next door with me.' Pat was only too glad to oblige. What were flowers when Ian Casson called?

'He says Mrs Tremaine can go home on Monday,' she told Kate when she returned. 'I've made a note on her record.'

'Has Mr Casson gone?' demanded Kate, who had only just come off the phone.

'Yes, he has.' What was wrong with Sister, biting her head off like that? Pat wondered. 'He saw Mrs Bealer, but only for a minute, and then he went charging off.'

'Okay, thank you.' Kate took the notes. It was just on

four p.m., and most likely, by now, Ian was meeting Helen down in the main entrance. They would be walking out into the brilliant June sunshine for tea.

A week later he told Mrs Bealer that her waiting time was over. He would be operating on Saturday morning. 'After which, Mrs Bealer, you'll be well on the way to recovery, and in three weeks or so, you'll be back with your family, feeling your old self once more.'

Janet Bealer said very little, except, 'I see,' and, 'Thank you, sir.' But half an hour later she called to him as he passed by her open door. He retraced his steps and went into her room. What she said then took him aback. He reasoned with her to no avail, then he went in search of Kate, who was at the ward desk, deciphering a nursing report.

'Can you spare a minute, Sister . . . in the office, if you will?' Turning, he strode back down the ward, leaving her to follow. As he neared the doors his gaze alighted on the sleeping form of Miss Norton, Helen's old nurse, who was just back from theatre. He had enquired how the old lady was, and Bill Jarman had told him, 'She'll do.' Meantime, Norty wasn't his problem, but Janet Bealer was. 'She won't sign the consent form for surgery unless you agree to be with her for the whole of the time she's down in theatre,' he told Kate in the office.

'I know she *threatened* not to sign,' Kate chewed on her underlip, 'but I thought when it came to it . . .'

'She needs this operation.' Ian's face was intent. 'Is there any chance of you doing what she asks . . . doing what she *demands*? I could arrange it with Sister Theatre, if you could absent yourself from the ward. Have you seen a hypophysectomy performed?'

'No, never,' she shook her head.

'Then it might be of interest, even helpful, from your point of view . . . all that as well as being a comfort to our friend. She'll be fathoms deep under the anaes-thetic, and she knows that, of course, but she still wants to be sure that you'll be there. So what do you think?' A smile rucked his face, one thick fair eyebrow rose. Kate was incapable of thinking at all when he looked at her like that, so perhaps that was why her first answer gave a very wrong impression:

'I'm off duty at the weekend,' she said, 'Staff Nurse will be in charge.'

'Oh well, in that case, forget it.' Ian's hand slapped down on the desk. 'I'll go and see the woman again . . . damn it, she must see sense!'

'Mr Casson . . . sir . . . Ian, please wait!' Kate sprang to her feet. 'What I was going to say was, *as* I'm off duty on Saturday, my time is my own, I can do as I please, and I *would* like to come into theatre. Had I been on the ward and been up to my eyes, then it might have been more difficult. Even so, I would still have done my best.'

His face changed and he sat down. 'You need your off-duty, Kate. I've no right to ask you to give it up, no right at all.'

She smiled, she couldn't help it—because we're going, she thought, through exactly the same perform-ance as we did ten days ago, at his private rooms, before his patients arrived. I don't have to jump to do his bidding, yet inevitably I do. Still, I'll be doing *this* for Mrs Bealer. I care about her welfare, and her state of mind, I'm doing it for her. 'I would like to come,' she emphasised. 'What time do you want her in theatre?'

'She's down for nine-thirty.'

'Then I'll get here early, in time to prep her and everything. I'll have a word with Staff Nurse, I'll come as her supernumerary, up until lunchtime. You'll be over and done by then?'

'Yes, I will.' He still looked troubled. 'Kate, are you sure about this?'

'Absolutely.'

'It's good of you.' His hand moved as though to clasp hers, then it fell to his side and he moved away, muttering about some reports that he'd left lying around in pathology. 'I'll leave you to tell Mrs Bealer,' he called. Kate promised she would. The consent form was signed, and put with the theatre notes.

Everything conspired to make her late at the hospital on Saturday. She rose at five-thirty, and slamming her front door just after six, discovered that the Fiat wouldn't start. She dared not spend time tinkering with it, and she couldn't ask Ellis to help. His bedroom curtains were still drawn over; she would have to telephone the Smugglers' Arms, in the hope that the landlord's son, who ran a taxi, would be up and willing to take her to work. Hurrying back into the cottage, she dialled his number, and all she could get was a curious and continuous hooting sound. Once again she dared not linger, once again she hurried into the garden. Stopping only to drop her key through Ellis's letterbox —he was going to use her washing-machine, as there wasn't one at Pinnocks—she ran down the hill in the early morning mist.

Bob Nansock was not only up, but had just returned from St Mawgan. He would be only too pleased, he said, to take her along to the hospital. 'Had my old gran in there, last year, something wrong with her innards, but they got her right, and she's knocking ninety . . . wunnerful what they can do. Still, I don't need to tell *you* that, do I?' His chunky, young man's face, dark with stubble, for he had not yet shaved, turned to her admiringly, as he eased the black Volvo out of his yard.

He drove swiftly and well, there was little traffic at this very early hour. The mist was clearing, lifting in swathes, draping itself round the trees, skirting the hedges, sweeping the boulder-strewn fields. The Cornish landscape was like no other, it had so many faces. Kate turned up her collar and huddled into her cape.

The night staff were still on duty when she entered the ward corridor. There was a smell of soap and water, and early morning tea. She asked what kind of a night Mrs Janet Bealer had passed. 'Pretty fair, she's been asking for you ever since five o'clock,' the auxiliary replied, busy with TPRs.

Kate went to the side-ward and found Janet Bealer anxious to have her bath. She said she was feeling 'not too bad', but had missed her cup of tea. 'I'm afraid we can't help that,' Kate said, 'but if your mouth is dry, you can rinse it out, only don't swallow anything down.'

'I don't mind anything now you're here.' Mrs Bealer had dreaded today, but now that her operation was only two hours away, she was resigned to it, even geared to it . . . helped by another's presence . . . the presence of a slim young woman with encouraging hazel eyes smiling at her from under her Sister's cap.

Mrs Bealer's cap, which Kate popped on her head after she returned from the bathrooms, was plain cotton and completely hid her hair. A hospital gown replaced her own nightdress, her wedding ring was taped. She was checked and labelled . . . like a chicken, she thought, ready for the oven. But after her premedication injection she ceased to think at all, but just lay and drowsed and floated, and swung on a sea of euphoria. Vaguely she registered that Kate was there, sitting by her bed. She was warm and snug, apart from her mouth, which was dry . . . so dry. She moistened her lips and tried to speak, but only managed a mumble . . . why try, why bother . . . she began to float again.

The theatre porters came to collect her. She felt them moving her, felt extra blankets being tucked round her, felt herself being transferred on to something hard and different from her bed. And now she was being wheeled along. The sensation was very strange, when she opened her eyes she could see the ceiling sliding backwards over her head. She could hear very clearly, ultra-clearly, little sounds seemed loud: 'I'm not asleep, I'm still awake.' Had she said the words, or only thought them? She gripped Kate's fingers hard.

Kate winced, but didn't free herself. 'You're quite all right,' she said, as the lift bore them down to the theatre suite. Mrs Bealer was transferred to a theatre trolley, while Kate donned overshoes. Then she followed a young nurse to the changing rooms, where she put on a gown and mob cap. She tied on a mask, then made her way down a long, sterile-zone corridor, into one of the five anaesthetic rooms. Adam Hart, the anaesthetist, whom she knew by sight, was standing near the stretcher. He beckoned to her and she went forward, taking Mrs Bealer's hand.

'It's Sister again,' she told the patient.

'Wondered . . . where . . .'

'I'll be with you now, all the time.' Out of the corner of her eye Kate could see the syringe being filled. She knew it most likely held Pentothal, the anaesthetic agent. She watched Adam Hart tapping the back of the patient's other hand to encourage a suitable vein to rise.

'Just a small prick, that's all,' he said, bending to Mrs Bealer. The butterfly needle slid into the vein; he asked her to start to count; she got up to four, tried to say 'five', then lapsed into unconsciousness. 'Good,' he said. Kate relinquished her other hand.

Turning round, she saw that the room was filling up with people, all gowned and masked like herself, standing about in groups. Even in their swaddled state, she could recognise one or two—Ian's registrar, the big-busted blonde, and the two young medical students who had come to the ward a week or ten days ago. The stretcher was wheeled through into the theatre and everyone followed it in. The patient was laid on the table and covered with drapes.

There was a hushed murmur of: 'Good morning, sir,' as Ian Casson walked in, looking bulkier in his green gown, face three-quarters concealed. His gaze swept over the assembly of people, alighting on the students. 'Better come and stand over here, hadn't you? You won't see much from there. You, too, Sister Browning.' Kate jumped when she heard her name; it seemed so shocking to hear it spoken in this rarefied atmosphere. She made no reply, but followed the students to Ian's side of the table. A blood transfusion was started, and he reached for the first instrument; Mrs Bealer's operation had begun.

Kate lost all sense of time, as she watched and concentrated on every stage of the delicate surgery. Everyone was quiet, the loudest sound was the metallic clink of instruments. Ian's voice, in contrast, seemed muted as he spoke, at times to Sister, and at times to the students, and at times to Adam Hart. He sutured the wound, then a splint of gauze soaked in collodion was applied to the nose and both nostrils were lightly packed. 'Keep her lying on her side, continue the infusion with dextrose and normal saline,' Kate heard him say; after which Mrs Bealer was gently transferred from the table and wheeled through into the recovery room next door. He thanked Sister Myner and her team for their help, stripped off his mask and gloves, and went out en route for the changing rooms. Kate watched him go; he smiled at Mrs Weiss and put a hand on his houseman's shoulder. They turned the corner, and she stared at the green-tiled wall.

'A perfect gentle knight, is he not?' Sister Myner said at her elbow.

'Mr Casson? Oh, yes, I suppose he is.' Kate felt her face going red. How hot these beastly mob caps were! She jerked hers off, loosening the tapes at the back of her high-necked gown.

'Come and have some coffee with us, along in our Common Room?' Sister Myner was young—big-toothed and healthy, with a skin like a damask rose. She tugged at Kate's arm. 'Do come, you look fit to drop.'

'Actually I'm not, just a little stiff, and thank you all the same, but I think I ought to have coffee with my staff nurse on the ward. There are one or two things I want to discuss with her.' She wouldn't go to the Common Room, Ian might be there, for in theatre block there was less segregation of ranks. Doctors and nurses and surgeons quite often all sat down together for coffee and tea, she knew that for a fact. And I couldn't face it at the moment, she thought, leaving the theatres floor with a feeling of relief and anticlimax mixed.

Once back on Penhallow, she went in search of Nurse Solly, whose task it had been to prepare Mrs Bealer's bed in the big main ward. She had got to be in there now for maximum surveillance; a post-op tray was laid up at the side. After she had made sure everything was there, Kate went into the office. Staff had had some coffee brought in for her.

'What was it like . . . riveting?' asked Joan True. She liked Kate, but she also liked to be fully in charge. She had never known Sister Stubbs to come in on her off-duty days, and no one could have been more conscientious than her.

'It was very interesting,' Kate replied, 'and this coffee is terrific—I needed it, my throat was like a husk.'

'How long are you here for?'

'I'll be off as soon as Janet Bealer comes up.'

Joan True flushed. 'Oh, I didn't mean . . .'

'You did, and I don't blame you. I wouldn't have come at all if Mr Casson hadn't asked me.'

'He probably wanted you to see him in action,' said Joan.

'I doubt that very much. It was Mrs Bealer, really, laying down conditions.' The phone rang then and, just in time, Kate stopped herself reaching for it. Staff was in charge, it was up to her; she watched her answer it. Joan True wasn't married, she lived at home with her father. Will I be like her at fifty? Kate wondered. Well, no, of course I won't. I'm a Ward Sister now, and by fifty I shall have moved a good deal higher. Why hadn't Joan tried for promotion? She was a good, diligent nurse. But she might not, of course, be the ambitious kind.

Mrs Bealer came up from the second floor just before twelve-thirty. She was transferred to her waiting bed and positioned flat on her side. She was very drowsy, but she knew Kate, who smiled down at her. 'You're absolutely fine, Mrs Bealer, safely back in your bed—it's all over, no need to worry now.' The faint pressure of her hand on Kate's was Janet Bealer's response. Kate sat with her till she slept, then left the ward.

She had no car, she remembered. She would get a bus from Tor Street, leaving the hospital precinct from the west gate. She walked through the corridor of Mather Wing, whose exit led into a square, flanked by the Path Labs and Haematology.

She never knew what caused her to trip—a gap in the

paving, perhaps, or because she was wearing loose sandals, or because, some distance ahead, she had seen Ian, turning the corner from Haem. He saw her too. He stopped and waited, and she increased her pace . . . and tripped. It was the kind of trip where one flounders and flails, fights to regain one's balance, and just at that moment . . . that exact moment . . . one of the windows in Path swung open on its metal arm, and her forehead struck the glass. The sound it made was still in her ears as she lay on the ground . . . she was being lifted, she was sitting against a wall, and two people were there. One was Ian, the other was round and red and apologetic. 'I had no idea anyone was there,' he was saying. Ian cautioned her to sit still. He looked at the big contusion above her right eye.

'I'm sorry, Sister . . . I'm just very sorry!' The red cherubic face belonged to a young pathologist, who looked more and more upset. 'I just opened the window, I didn't expect . . .'

'Do you always *fling* your windows open, Doctor?' Ian's voice was curt, and it had the effect of jerking Kate out of her daze. With his arm about her she got to her feet, and found one sandal was missing. The young doctor brought it to her, and as she put it on she felt the pain stiffening her head. 'You're going to have an egg-sized lump!' Once more Ian looked at the bruise. 'I'll take you along to the Accident Unit and we'll get an X-ray done. You've not broken the skin surface, which is something, I suppose.'

'But I may have cracked my skull . . . that's charming!' Kate resorted to sarcasm, trying to hide the anxiety she felt. Supposing she had got a fracture . . . supposing . . . supposing . . . supposing she couldn't nurse for several weeks?

'There's nothing you can do,' she heard Ian telling the

perspiring young doctor. 'I think she's all right, but I want to make sure. You get back inside.'

'Will you let me know?'

'Enquire in Cas, say I gave you permission.' He was at his most dominant when anxious and vexed.

Good of him to be worried about me, Kate thought bemusedly, glad of his grip on her arm as they crossed the yard to Casualty. Her knees felt weak—perhaps she'd cracked those too!

Casualty was busy; well, of course it was; it was the last week in June, the last week of a heatwave June, and a Saturday afternoon. Most of the waiting patients were children with sprains and cuts; there were adults with sunburn, old people with fainting attacks. Bypassing the big reception desk, Ian sat Kate down and went in search of Harold Formby, the Casualty Officer. She was soon through in X-Ray, where three films were taken. 'No bony injury,' Harold Formby said, letting her see the results. 'We'll give you some pain-killing tablets, then you'll have to go home and rest. You should be all right tomorrow, but you'll have a nasty bruise.' He held a mirror up to her face, not that she needed one, for she could actually see the swelling on her forehead simply by turning her eyes in an upwards direction; it was like a bulging roof. 'It'll be down tomorrow,' Harold Formby was cheerful, 'but the colour of blue-black ink, and after that you'll see green and yellow hues.'

'Thanks for the forecast!' Kate's tone was wry. Harold patted her shoulder. One of the nurses fetched her tablets, and gave her a pair of dark glasses. She was grateful for the latter, and she slipped them on, for bright sunlight and aching heads have a habit of not mixing very well.

'You can't drive home,' Ian declared, his hand cupping her elbow as he steered her over the floor to the exit doors. 'I've finished here now, so I'll take you. We'll use your car, if you like. I can walk back from Poldenack, or get a taxi . . . that way you'll have your car at the right end, as soon as you're fit to drive.'

'There's something wrong with the Fiat,' she told him, 'I didn't drive in today—that's how I came to be walking along past the pathology labs. I was making my way to the nearest bus stop. I'd still like to go home by bus,' she added firmly, facing him on the steps.

'What on earth for?' His look was incredulous.

'I like travelling by bus.' She stared across the yard at a waiting ambulance; she didn't really see it, just registered that it was there. She was only aware of the man in front of her.

'Now look . . .' she heard the burst of annoyance, the impatience in his voice, 'I'm suggesting I drive you home, Kate, and drive you home I will. And that, incidentally, is *all* I'm suggesting, there's no need to safeguard yourself. You drew a very neat line between us two weeks ago, remember? So come on, don't be a silly girl.'

Had she felt herself, had her head not been aching, she would never have given in. As it was, the thought of a smooth drive home instead of a jolty one overcame all else for the moment. 'I'm not seven years old, you know!' she snapped with a touch of defiance, even then.

'Then don't behave as though you are.' This was not said nastily, it was said with affection, and Kate felt every one of her barriers rocking. Apart from anything else, I like him, but then I always did, was her last thought before she got into his car.

He talked very little as they crossed the city, which was crowded with Saturday shoppers. There was a big covered market; she could see its roof, hear the stallholders' calls. 'Comfortable?' Ian asked her once, glancing at her briefly.

'Superbly so, thank you. This is a lovely car.'

'Yours is a Fiat?'

'Yes, it was Danny's.'

'Which makes it precious, no doubt.'

'Yes, it does. It's also easy to drive,' she said quietly, adding nothing more.

He knew she was living at Aubyns, she had told him so earlier on. He remembered Rose speaking about the cottage . . . scoffing a little, too. 'We spent all our holidays there, as kids, when Granny was alive. Kate adored it, but I didn't. It was poky and smelled of mice.' 'Don't you get lonely at the cottage?' he asked Kate now.

'Not at all. I love it. I enjoy my own company at times.'

'Even so,' he passed a van, 'it's not all that good a thing to be on your own when you're not feeling well. Suppose you were ill?'

'I have good health, and I don't make a habit of having accidents, and much though I love my job, I wouldn't want to live near it, *too* near it—say in the Sisters' Home. I like to get away when I've finished, I like my own place, and my garden, and everything. Don't you feel that about your house?'

They halted at the lights, and Ian turned his head. 'It's different for a man.'

'Oh, for heaven's sake . . . oh, *really*!' she exclaimed. 'What a chauvinist remark!'

'Don't belabour me, Kate!' His hand covered hers as it lay on her lap. She felt the familiar leap of her senses, and a following drive of panic.

'Tell me about Mrs Bealer,' she blurted out.

His expression changed, so did the lights, and as the

car moved forward his hand left hers:

'Did everything go as planned?' she persisted gently.

'Yes . . . yes, I think so,' he took his cue from her. 'I'm very pleased, and grateful to you for giving up your morning.'

Politeness could hide so many things; she felt on firmer ground. 'I'm the one to be grateful,' she said, 'it helps with the nursing care when one can see what goes on in theatre.'

'Did you say you're *not* on duty tomorrow?'

'I'm not, it's my weekend off.'

'Well, I'm glad about that, at least.' There was subtle emphasis on the last words. The atmosphere sparked once again, and Kate stared out of the window, trying to hinge her mind and thoughts on the lines of houses and bungalows stretching out as far as the eye could see. There was no more conversation, just the faint hum of the car, but as the Bay came into view, blue and crescent-shaped, Ian said, easing his sun-flap down: 'You're going to have to direct me. I'm afraid I don't know Poldenack all that well.'

They dropped down into the little town, taking the harbour road. The sea heaved and swelled on their left, making Kate feel queasy; she stared ahead and tried not to look at it: 'Go straight up the hill by the Smugglers' Arms . . . there, by those striped umbrellas.' She pointed quickly and Ian swung for the turn. And now they had their backs to the sea, and the car was climbing steadily. 'Those are the cottages,' she pointed again, 'mine is the second one.'

'Heavens above!' he ejaculated, 'you'll catch all the wind up there.'

'That's true, yes, but there's not been a really bad gale since I've been here. And the cottage is strong, I remember my grandmother saying how solid it was.' As the big car thrust up the hill, she saw Ellis in her garden, moving one way, then the other, sloping slightly forward. She had forgotten his promise to mow her lawn, but she knew why he was doing it—as a quid pro quo for the use of her washing-machine. He hated being under an obligation, it was almost a fetish with him. She rather admired him for it, in a way.

'Is that your gardener?' she heard Ian ask, which made her start to laugh, then quickly stop, because the movement hurt her head.

'No, it certainly isn't. It's Ellis . . . Ellis Rand, the author. I told you about him, remember. I bought his book—you saw it when I . . . when I came to your house.'

'I didn't know he was here . . . in *Cornwall*!' His face showed astonishment.

'He's renting the cottage next door. Perhaps you would like to come in and meet him?' Her hand reached down and unfastened her safety-belt.

'Well, yes . . . yes, all right, I will.' He didn't sound very certain. He leaned across and opened her door, then got out himself. Seeing the car, Ellis came to the gate, his eyes going straight to Kate's head.

'What's happened?' he exclaimed.

'Nothing much, I'll tell you in a minute.' She introduced him to Ian, and watched the two men shake hands. They looked so different standing there—Ian fair and tall, Ellis thinner, his thistledown hair lying flat for once; there was a grass stain on the leg of his best cream jeans. They were muttering the usual pleasantries, Ellis looking at Kate.

'How did it happen?' He meant her head, and he turned to Ian again.

'Not in the car, don't look so accusing!' Kate pushed through the gate. 'I tripped in the hospital yard and hit a window on the way down. There's no real damage done, it's not as bad as it looks.'

'It looks bad enough.' He took her arm and they began to walk up the path. 'Come and sit down, I've got lunch ready, I thought we'd eat outside. Are you sure you're all right, are you positive?' He looked at her again.

Their words floated back to Ian as he stood at the gate. He looked at the cottage in front of them, built of stone and slate. He looked at the one next door, which nudged it. He could see against the hedge—on Kate's side—a table laid for two. There was a line of washing, male garments hung motionless in the heat, over the uniform stripes of the freshly-cut lawn. 'I'll say goodbye,' he called out, and the two of them turned round.

'Oh, Ian,' Kate came back to him, 'have a drink before you go—a long, cool squash, if you like. But perhaps you're in a hurry,' she countered quickly, seeing him shade his head. Her own head was muzzy now, and she wanted to get indoors. At the moment she wanted nothing more than to sit down and be quiet. She lip-read his brief reply:

'That's kind, but I ought to get back.'

'Thank you again for bringing me home.'

'My pleasure,' she thought he said, as Ellis rejoined them, slipping his hand once more within her arm. 'I'm sure you'll see that she rests, Mr Rand.'

'Of course.' Ellis blinked in surprise. He thought the Casson fellow was high-handed, dishing out his orders. 'Naturally I'll look after Kate.' He tightened his grip on her arm.

'Good.' Ian turned to his car and got in. A gull screamed overhead. Standing there on the cottage path, still feeling rather dazed, Kate watched the big white car till it passed from sight.

After lunch in the garden—a quiche which Ellis had bought at the supermarket—he went back to his cottage to work, leaving Kate on her lounger. 'I'll be back at five with a tray of tea, so don't get up until then. It's a terrible bruise, Kate, really shocking,' he bent down and peered at her, 'I've never seen anything likc it in my life!'

'You're cheering me up no end,' she said, pulling a wry face. But in actual fact she was touched by his concern. Up till now she had tended to think of Ellis as egocentric, wrapped up in his own affairs, as single men often were, but he had proved her wrong this afternoon. He had even, he said, managed to get her car to go . . . something to do with the plugs. He had heard her trying to start it, and looked at it during the morning. It was good of him. She lay in the garden and drowsed.

Even so, thoughts of Ian encroached, filtered through layers of consciousness—real and semi—preventing total rest. Opening her eyes, Kate saw the scene in the garden as he must have done—Ellis mowing the lawn, looking at home, the table set for two, Ellis's protective manner, the cottage door standing open, Ellis going in and out at will. Had Ian thought she and Ellis were close? Had he read those signs quite wrongly? It was possible he had; on the other hand, he might not have noticed *or* cared. His abrupt departure might just have been a perfectly reasonable wish to salvage what he could of his afternoon.

Abandoning sleep, she found her handbag and took out a letter from Rose. It had come the day before, and she began to read it again. It contained mainly family news, it told Kate how she was feeling, *and* looking . . . 'enormous, darling . . . only three months to go! Hugh says I've never looked lovelier, he's such a wonderful man. Oh, Kate, I wish you'd marry again . . . surely you loathe being single? I know you're ambitious, and want to get on, I know you love your job, but you could have both if you played your cards right . . . a husband and a career. As you know, I didn't want to keep working.' Rose had left the Walbrook the day after the split with Ian; then until she married Hugh, she had worked as a temp at another hospital.

The letter went on to mention Ian, for Kate had told Rose about him—how she had come to meet him again, and how he had a girl-friend, Helen Reever, who owned a flower shop. 'I was riveted to hear about Ian,' Rose wrote, 'and so, of course, was Hugh. I'm glad he's got a steady girl-friend, but I doubt if he'll marry her.'

And she hopes he won't, Kate thought, folding the letter in two, for in her heart of hearts she likes to think, even though she's happy with Hugh, that Ian still loves her, still dreams about her, still can't bring himself to put any other female in her place.

CHAPTER FIVE

ON Monday Kate was on lates duty, from lunchtime till eight p.m.; everyone commented on her bruise, starting with Staff Nurse True, who gave her a concise résumé on each of the patients before leaving the ward for the afternoon. 'There's a new patient in the side-ward,' she said as she neared the end of the list, 'a Miss Sawyer, broken nose, deviated septum. She was brought into the Accident Department at midnight on Saturday. Mr Casson operated on Sunday morning, then she came up to us—no great beauty, with her nose in splints and two black eyes! To look at the two of you, Sister,' Staff stared at Kate's purpling bruise, 'one would think you'd been fighting each other, indulging in fisticuffs!'

'Which would make more exciting reading than just bumping into a window,' said Kate, reading Miss Sawyer's notes. 'How did she come to break her nose?'

'Fell off her bike coming home from a party—and no, she wasn't drunk. Her wheel struck a stone, or a kerb, or something; anyway, she came off. You'll like her, she's easy, hates giving any trouble. Mr Casson's seeing her at four today, he rang up earlier on.'

'I see.' Kate's mouth had a papery feel; she swallowed and moistened her teeth. 'And how's Janet Bealer?'

'I'm coming to her.' Staff picked up the last of the folders. 'Mr Casson saw her yesterday, seemed very pleased with her. He may want the drip discontinued today, and the nasal packs removed. He rang up this morning, and I gave him the latest report on Evelyn

Sawyer. I think he was really expecting to have a word with you.'

'Providing the person in charge knows her job, he doesn't mind who it is,' said Kate. 'He wouldn't suffer fools gladly, though, he's not the forbearing sort.'

'No, I don't think he is.' Joan True got up, then sat down again. 'Oh, there's one more—Miss Norton, the hiatus hernia case. Now she, I think, would win a gold medal for the fastest recovering patient. Just look at her now, just *look*, Sister!' They glanced through the viewing window just in time to see Adela Norton, Helen Reever's old nurse, struggling manfully to reach the ward doors en route for the bathrooms and loos. She was able to wear her own nightclothes now, which were striped men's pyjamas, floppy and loose, tied at the waist with tapes. She wore no dressing-gown, nothing on her feet, and she walked with a rubber-tipped stick. She fiercely resisted all efforts to help her, she was waving Nurse Heston aside. Her mouth was clenched, her eyes glimmered black under her mushroom hairstyle; Miss Norton was nothing, but *nothing* like anyone's nurse. She had had the operation called Boerema's, a fairly simple one. Nevertheless, simple or not, it had been major surgery, and Adela Norton had been magnificent.

'To think,' said Kate, 'when we heard she was coming, we expected a sweet old lady, apple-cheeked and soft-voiced—' Miss Norton's voice was stentorian—'it just goes to show one should never expect people to fit into slots, or be true to the type we think they ought to be.'

'I'm off, and not sorry to be going, either. It's seemed a very long morning, longer than usual.' Joan True stretched, pulling off her cap.

''Bye, Joan, many thanks.' Kate read through one or two notes, then started the drugs round, calling Nurse

Solly to help. This was the round that gave her the chance to speak with every patient. It was a learning round for Nurse Solly too . . . teaching was part of Kate's job. 'If Mr Casson decides he wants Mrs Bealer's packs removed and her drip taken down, you'd better come and watch,' she told the girl. On the whole she was very pleased with Marian Solly's progress. Since the Proudman incident she had not had occasion to upbraid her about anything—much to her own and to Nurse Solly's relief.

Staff had been right when she said Kate would like Evelyn Sawyer. It took courage to laugh when your nose was firmly clamped in a plaster splint, and you had the type of eyes called 'shiners', but Evelyn managed it. 'With my clown's nose, I should be in a circus, not a hospital bed!' She swallowed the analgesic tablets Kate dispensed from the trolley. Someone had plaited her long, blonde hair, and tied it with a tape. She stared at Kate's bruise, but didn't remark on it.

'We match in certain respects, don't we?' said Kate, catching her eye.

'When will the bruises disappear?' asked Evelyn.

'Do you mean yours or mine?'

'Mine, I'm afraid, I'm the selfish kind!'

'Yours will fade off quickly. The surgeon who set your nose will be in this afternoon. I should think you're likely to be with us for about a week or ten days, depending, of course, on what Mr Casson says.'

'So long as I don't look this awful for ever!'

'You won't, I promise you,' Kate assured her.

'I'm a beauty consultant at Asterfords Store. What could be more incongruous!'

'I agree, not a lot,' Kate laughed. 'How did the accident happen?' She drew up a chair and prepared to listen, knowing that very often patients were helped by talking about themselves. By the time she left the side-ward the librarian had arrived.

'All right to go in, is it, Sister?' Mrs Mainer was brawny and tall, which was just as well, because her bookcase-on-wheels was heavy and cumbersome. As Kate helped her guide it through the ward she saw that Helen Reever was sitting at Miss Norton's bedside, and she felt a prick of annoyance. The girl had a nerve; she knew Monday was a non-visiting day. She should have asked permission before she went into the ward.

'You don't mind, do you, Sister,' she said as Kate approached, 'but you weren't in your room when I came in. I *did* put my head round and look.'

'You can have a few minutes but, please, not more. Miss Norton needs to rest.'

'Oh, send her out, Sister, if you want to . . . rules are meant to be kept.' Miss Norton gave an admonishing sweep of the hand in Helen's direction. 'Because she's a friend of Mr Casson it shouldn't mean advantages.'

'Especially . . .' said Kate, surprising even herself by her acid tongue, 'especially as, in the ordinary way, Mr Ian Casson has very little to do with this hospital!' She knew she looked angry, she could feel her face flaming; both women stared at her. Miss Norton searched for a tissue and blew her nose.

'I'll go in a few minutes, I promise.' Helen's tone was beguiling. 'Actually, I came to bring that.' She pointed to Miss Norton's locker, on the top of which sat a white-framed photograph. Out of politeness, and contrition for her outburst, Kate bent to look at it. She saw that it was a photograph of Helen coming out of her shop with her arms full of golden daffodils. Somehow or other her curly-mop hair took the colour of the flowers; her track suit was green; she was smiling into the lens. 'Ian took it.' There was pride and satisfaction in Helen's voice.

'It's very good.' Kate managed to smile.

'It's a *clever* photograph,' Miss Norton corrected, looking from one to the other of their faces. 'Helen's not photogenic, so he must have had to pose her carefully. Whereas you, Sister,' she fastened on Kate, 'would be an easy subject. You're not pretty like Helen, but your bones are good, and your looks, such as they are, are the durable kind, they'll last you all your life.'

'That's good to know!' Kate couldn't help laughing. Helen pulled a face.

'Norty's compliments are the two-edged kind,' she remarked to Kate in the office. She had followed her in there. She was hanging about, waiting for Ian again, or so Kate supposed, but how could she oust her without being downright rude? 'But I should imagine,' Helen went on, 'that you *would* be photogenic. I would love to have your kind of cheekbones, I'd adore to be tall and thin. Was your husband tall?'

'Yes, he was.' The question took Kate by surprise.

'It must have been awful losing him,' mused Helen. 'I can't imagine it. I can't see myself in a like position —I've never lost anyone close. Ian told me about it . . . told me he knew you before he came down here. I know about your sister too.'

'That's all past history,' shrugged Kate.

'Oh heavens, I realise that!' Helen said. 'Ian's no actor, what he feels he shows, if you know how to read him aright.'

Kate was staring blankly at her, trying to say something apt, when Ian came in; she held out his clean white coat.

'You here again, Nell?' He buttoned the coat, looking over at Helen. His greeting was hardly effusive, and his mood was a thorny one. Kate saw this at once, as he briefly acknowledged her. He turned round to look at her bruise, hands hanging straight at his sides, knees bent to bring his height to hers. 'Seems to be running its colourful course. No headache now, I hope?'

'None at all.' She wished he would drop his hectoring, bossy manner.

'And you're well, are you?'

'Yes, perfectly well.'

'I'm off now, Ian,' Helen broke in, 'thank you for letting me see Norty, Kate.' He opened the door wide, and she went off without a backward glance.

'And now to work.' He picked up two Kardex from the desk. 'Mrs Bealer first, I think,' he turned to the nursing report. 'We'll have her drip down and that packing out, which will make her more comfortable.'

'Can Nurse Solly watch? It would be instructive. I've had a trolley laid up.' Kate tried to add the formal 'sir', but the word seemed to stick in her throat.

'Of course she can, we all have to learn . . . *one* way or another.' His tone was cryptic, but his look was bland, directed straight into her eyes. It was the kind of look one couldn't latch on to; it was unassailable . . . just a blue regard, edging her to the ward.

He was different when he spoke to Mrs Bealer, he was gentleness itself, changing his overlord style to his bed-side one. He stood at the foot of her bed while Kate removed the packs. He heard her reassuring the patient, heard her instructing Nurse Solly, saw her clamp the infusion tube and remove the cannula from the vein in Mrs Bealer's arm. 'You'll feel more easy now, Mrs Bealer. We'll bring you a drink in a minute.' She told Nurse Solly to remove the trolley, and reminded her about her fluids. 'You'll find her balance chart at the back of her notes.'

Ian had a brief word with the patient, as Kate swung back the curtains. 'She's settled better in the main ward than I thought,' he said afterwards. 'It helps having her in there, does it?' He turned round on Kate, as they left the ward and entered the corridor.

'It makes observation that much easier,' she agreed.

'That's what I meant. You've seen Miss Sawyer?' He wasted no words.

'Yes, sir, I have.'

'With Mrs Tremaine and Miss Clifford gone,' he said, after a pause, 'may I bring another patient into the second side-ward next week, for labyrinthectomy? She's a Miss Elder, aged sixty-three, suffering from Ménière's disease. She's very debilitated by vertigo and sickness, and I want to do something for her.'

'Of course, admit her.' The question he asked could only be answered one way—firmly in the affirmative —he knew that, and so did she. Enquiring from her was a mere politeness, because she knew that he would have gone through all the proper channels, Miss Rone being one of them. Still, he had bothered to mention it, he had given her plenty of warning; he was a courteous man, and what more could she ask?

Miss Elder came in Monday, and on Tuesday William Jarman admitted a patient for cholecystectomy. And tomorrow (Kate checked the list) Miss Norton would be going out—not, however, to her own house as yet; she was spending two weeks at the hospital's convalescent home just outside Tintagel. William Jarman had told her this was sensible.

She was in the day room playing Patience; when she saw Kate come in, she scooped up her cards, sighing with frustration and clicking her tongue. 'I can't seem to concentrate. That's what illness does for you, Sister . . . gives you a brain like a piece of wet sponge cake!'

'You'll feel entirely different when you've had your holiday.' Kate picked one of her cards up off the floor.

'You may be right,' the old lady conceded, 'you may be right, at that. I'm getting used to being a patient—I'm even getting used to hospital food, disgusting though it is.'

'How are you getting to Tintagel?' asked Kate. 'Are you having hospital transport?'

'Mr Casson is driving me.' The look she directed at Kate was rapier-sharp. 'He and Helen are taking me, making a day of it. They don't get all that much off-time, they're both busy people. Running a business like Helen does is no sinecure.'

'I'm sure not.' Kate longed to escape, but something held her there, tensed to hear more, yet wishing to turn a deaf ear.

'She's young too—about your age, perhaps?'

'I'm twenty-five,' Kate supplied.

'Which is her age exactly.' Miss Norton sounded pleased. 'When I was twenty-five I was her mother's nurse, you know. She was lovely, a beautiful child . . . a Carrington, you know. When she grew up and married she had me to run the big house at Camborne, and when Helen was born I became her nurse, that made me very proud. They sold the house and went to America soon after Helen left school. At one time I thought she might join them, but she never speaks of it now. She and Mr Casson are what you young people call "together".' Her words dropped softly, like one of her playing cards.

'I don't really think we ought to be discussing them, Miss Norton.' Kate made a movement backwards towards the door.

Miss Norton laughed. 'Oh, nonsense, girl! I'm giving nothing away. Anyone with eyes to see could recognise the signs. I'm fond of them both, I hope they'll marry, but I also realise one has to move with the times, and young adults please themselves. I still think marriage is best for a girl. Helen is pretty and rich. She's an only child, and one day, of course . . .'

Kate had heard enough. She turned away and turned her back. 'Mr Casson has come,' she said. He was standing at the ward doors holding them open, stretching his arms out wide to help Evelyn Sawyer, who was bringing the tea trolley in. Eve was always helping with something, she liked to be occupied, and the patients enjoyed having someone new around. The bruises round her eyes had faded, but she still wore the splint on her nose. Her hair had been washed and hung straight to her waist in a golden waterfall. She was asking Ian when her splint could come off.

'Tomorrow,' he said, 'just during the day, but put it back on at night. I think we can discharge you on Thursday, then you'll need to attend the Fracture Clinic about twice, that's all, and then you'll be all right.'

'Thank you for all you've done for me,' she said.

'You've been a model patient.' He seemed perfectly happy to stand by her trolley, drinking the tea she had poured him, and munching a biscuit, one of the sort he liked. He saw Kate coming, but didn't move. 'Hello, Sister, how are things?'

'Oh, fine, just fine,' she said, smiling all over her face. Her tone was flippant; she wasn't acting so much as overreacting to Miss Norton's words, to her little cachet of news. She wondered why it should trouble her so, turn like a screw in her chest, and feel so painful . . . more and more painful, as she looked back at Ian.

What Adela Norton had let slip was no real surprise. She had always thought that he and Helen were having an affair. But suspecting was different from knowing, suspecting left room for doubt. There was no doubt now,

she had to face that, what she had heard was true. Miss
Norton was artful, watchful and sharp, but she wasn't
the type to lie. She would never demean herself to lie
. . . and she told me the truth on purpose; it was no slip
she meant me to know . . . she's guessed I'm attracted to
Ian, Kate thought. How dreadful . . . oh, how awful!
She bit hard on her lip . . . just for a second the floor did
a sideways tip.

'Are you all right?' Ian's hand on her arm brought the
ward rushing back into focus, and with it anger; she
stepped back and wrenched her arm free.

'Yes, of *course* I'm all right! How many *more* times
. . . why all this *sickening* fuss!' Her voice was low, yet it
seemed to boom and reverberate back at her.

His face stiffened, the lines on it lengthened, his
mouth opened slightly. 'I'm sorry I enquired!' The
childish retort brought the sting of tears to her eyes. For
goodness' sake, what am I trying to do . . . make him
hate my guts? she thought.

'I'll be in the office when you're ready,' he said; a
nerve twitched at his jaw, his eyes were hostile. Kate felt
utterly miserable. She knew he had gone, she heard the
ward doors snuff to behind him. Eve was studiously
avoiding her eyes; she must have heard her outburst.
Kate felt ashamed. She must join him in her room. 'I'm
here to see Miss Elder,' was all he said when she entered
the office.

'The Menière's patient . . . oh, yes, of course.' She
dived for the filing cabinet.

'I've got her notes, I helped myself.' She heard him
turning the pages. 'I'm off tomorrow, so I shan't be here,
but my Registrar will come, or Paul Kyber, depending
on how they're fixed. Miss Elder is first on my list for
Wednesday, so one of the anaesthetists will be along
tomorrow early on.'

'Yes, I see.' The carpet was worn, the pattern hardly showed, except at the edges where red and green threaded along in scrolls. Ian was standing on the worn part, and Kate stared down at his shoes—black and shiny, and starting to move, he was going towards the door. 'I'm sorry I was so rude just now. It was quite unjustified.' She looked at him and found him looking at her.

'Yes, I think it was, but you're overworked, I realise that, of course. Let us see Miss Elder and then I'll get off, and leave you to your ploys.' He was already walking away from her, opening the side-ward door. She heard him greet Miss Elder, heard her faint reply, before she managed to move from the office, gather her wits and her courage, and follow him . . . as Sister on the ward.

All through the following day, when Miss Norton was discharged, when Annika Weiss came to see Miss Elder, when a new patient was admitted, Kate asked herself why she should feel that she had bludgeoned to death something that could have grown to magic between Ian and herself. It's ridiculous to feel like that, he belongs to Helen Reever, she reminded herself. Oh, he looked at me, yes, looked with intent, but nothing was really meant. It probably amused him to try it on, to dally with Rose's sister—the little widow, who might be feeling low. That was all it was, you've killed nothing at all, so stop feeling so regretful, and so 'if only', and get on with your work.

A shuffling sound at her open door made her pull out of her thoughts. 'I've come for a chat,' said Mrs Polden, depositing her girth, which was more than considerable, on to Kate's spare office chair.

Mrs Polden was the new patient, and she was in for a cholecystectomy—removal of gall-bladder, due to the presence of stones. Mr Jarman had insisted she be put on a special low-calorie diet, to get her weight well down before surgery. It had been useless to ask her to do this at home, she needed supervision. She was one of those people who thought she knew best in any situation. She had been an in-patient for a very short time, yet already she had proffered unwanted advice to all the nurses and most of the patients too. 'What I always say is . . .' had been going on for hours.

'What can I do for you?' asked Kate, putting down her pen.

Mrs Polden puffed and loosened her housecoat. 'Nothing, I just feel like company. They all want to rest in there.' Her newly permed head nodded forward, indicating the ward.

'It's the rest time, Mrs Polden. We try to keep it quiet.' Kate felt a little sorry for her, she looked so out of place, and ill too . . . one couldn't lose sight of that. 'Why don't you lie on your bed and read, or have your radio on, using your head-phones—lots of patients do?'

'Never had anything to do with hospitals . . . takes some getting used to.'

'Nearly everyone feels like that when they first come in.' Kate got to her feet. 'Look, my dear, I'm going through into the ward. Why not come with me and try to rest? I'll find you some magazines.'

'Trying to get rid of me, are you?' Mrs Polden's lip jutted out.

'Of course not,' Kate smiled, helping her up from the chair. 'But you know how it is, there are jobs to be done—Penhallow is a very big ward. I'll come and talk to you later on, after visiting time. I expect you'll be having a visitor?'

'My boy and girl'll come . . . both out of work, can't get jobs.' She leaned heavily on Kate's arm. 'And they don't take a blind bit of notice of me, think they know it all. Oh . . . oh, sorry, love!' she gave a hiccoughing cough. She had cannoned into little Miss Elder who was coming back from the bathrooms. 'So what's she in for?' she watched the small figure go into the second side-ward. 'Bad case, is she . . . looks half dead to me?'

'She's very far from that,' said Kate, sidetracking her question. After taking her into the ward and handing her over to Nurse Finn, she retraced her steps to the side-ward and went to see Miss Elder. She was probably feeling apprehensive, she was due for surgery tomorrow —an ear operation to cure her dizziness and resultant feeling of sickness. Miss Elder had been having a very rough time for a year.

She wasn't old, only just in her sixties, but ill-health made her seem older. She was a fluffy-haired, birdy little woman, who twittered when she talked. 'I'm nervous, but not frightened, Sister,' she was speaking about her op. 'Mr Casson has explained it to me so fully, he's been very kind and frank. He left the choice entirely to me, he didn't press nor persuade. I know that the hearing in the ear will go, but so will the dizziness. I can't tell you how awful that's been, how it pulls one down. I hear very well with my other ear, one can't expect to be perfect, not in middle-age . . . something's got to go.'

'I wish everyone was as acceptive as you,' Kate said as she got up to go. 'I'll leave your door slightly open, then you won't feel so alone.' Nurse Heston had already told her that Miss Elder had confessed to a mild degree of claustrophobia.

Next day she had her operation, and came through it very well. She was back in her bed and sleeping naturally shortly before midday. On Thursday Evelyn Sawyer went home, minus her splint. She looked as she always did, shiningly clean, hair drawn back in a tail, a red and white cotton dress swinging round her knees. Kate went down to the main entrance with her; a taxi was taking her home. She and Eve had arranged to meet one another from time to time. Eve had suggested it and Kate had agreed; she could do with a girl-friend to talk to. She was missing Rose and her friends in Surrey; she and Eve could get in some tennis, and swim, and walk, and visit each other's homes. Ellis was hardly ever available, Ellis was always busy . . . well, of course he was, that was why he was here.

'Thanks for everything,' Eve said now, climbing into her taxi. She lived in a flat over Asterfords Store.

'Thank you for coming!' They both laughed at that.

'See you!' Eve waved her hand.

The taxi drew off, and Kate went back to her ward.

CHAPTER SIX

THREE days after her operation Miss Caroline Elder began to have episodes of confusion, especially during the night. She had twice attempted to get out of bed, which was dangerous for her as yet, as she still had a residual dizziness.

Ian frowned as he read the night report, which Kate placed before him. 'Put cotsides up.' His tone was peremptory, and although she knew he was right, although she had every intention of doing what he said, his manner made her want to argue the point.

'She's mildly claustrophobic,' she told him.

'Cotsides won't affect that.' He was reading and didn't look up; he even shook his head in an irritated fashion, as though to brush her off.

Goaded, she ploughed on, determined to have her say. 'I've often found that confused patients are made even more confused by being railed in—Miss Elder would loathe it,' she insisted.

His head came up very slowly and he gave her a long, measured look. 'See that they're put up, please, Kate. Tell Miss Elder why—explain that they're for her own protection. I'm sure you'll find she'll see sense.'

'If she's as sensible as that she doesn't need them, she's rarely confused in the day.'

'Please do as I say,' he insisted quietly.

'Well, of course I will, but . . .'

'And now I would like to give you details of the patient taking Miss Sawyer's bed.' He proceeded to do so; and seething inside, Kate paid due attention. Sir Casson would have his way no matter what!

After he had gone, leaving her feeling as though she had brushed with a stranger, she did her best to explain to Miss Elder why it would be safer to have cotsides erected at her bed. She tempered the explanation with tact, even bent the truth a little. 'You're a restless sleeper, you see, Miss Elder. Apparently, in the night, you nearly rolled out on to the floor, so the rails will make you safe.' She deliberately refrained from saying 'cotsides', which might make her feel like an infant, or a geriatric, which was probably even worse. Nurses Heston and Solly put up the sides, and Miss Elder looked unhappy, but politely said that of course she understood.

'It's my opinion she doesn't need them,' Pat Finn, the agency nurse, remarked to Kate, as they did the medicine round. 'We can all keep an eye on her, leave her door open wide. We're in and out of the corridor a dozen times an hour.'

'Mr Casson is right to err on the safe side,' Kate said carefully. And she wondered, as she did so, why she should feel impelled to defend him to the others and —even more strangely—be annoyed with them for thinking his judgment was wrong.

'For two pins I'd take them down . . . when Sir's not around, that is,' she heard Nurse Heston expostulating to Zia in the kitchen.

'I know what you mean. She looked real upset when I took in her tea.' Zia was slicing bread with her customary panache, wielding the big steel knife like a cavalry sword. They both stopped talking when Kate came in. Zia carried on slicing, Nurse Heston went out and busied herself in the sluice.

Perhaps unwisely, Kate held back from taking them

up on their words. She didn't feel it was necessary, she trusted all her staff. They might air their views, disagree with orders, but they would never disobey them. They were loyal girls; so she said nothing, merely mentioning to Zia the matter of Mrs Polden who kept sneaking into the kitchen and eating biscuits . . . 'to fill up me aching void.'

'You must keep a closer watch, Zia. Put all the food away when you're not in the kitchen. She's on a strict diet, so of course she's hungry, poor soul. But if she doesn't lose weight as she should, then I'll have Mr Jarman to answer to.'

'All right, Sister, I'll watch it,' Zia reached for the butter, 'but I wouldn't put it past her visitors to slip her something in.'

'They were doing so, but now they're frisked before they go into the ward. It's embarrassing, but we have to do it, it's for her own good in the end.' Kate sighed a little; the last time the son had been downright offensive when asked to turn out his pockets, especially when bags of crisps and a slab of milk chocolate had been thrown on the desk, and confiscated by her. 'You can have them when you go home, Mr Polden,' she had tried to explain the position, but all he had done was curl his lip and swear at her again. She was beginning to realise that some of the things she had to do as Sister made her unpopular, even disliked . . . well, so be it, she thought; you knew it wouldn't be all beer and skittles; she used her father's expression, and she tried to laugh and disregard the chill of disillusionment that besets even the most stouthearted at times.

Ian's new patient, Mrs Flow, for tonsillectomy, was admitted to the second side-ward during the following week. An hour later the same afternoon an appendicitis case came in as an emergency sent up from A and EU.

She was a Mrs Romer, in great pain, febrile with a rapid pulse. 'I'm as sure as I can be that she's perforated,' William Jarman told Kate. 'There's a letter from her GP . . . here, read it,' he thrust it into Kate's hand. 'She's had nothing by mouth for twenty-four hours, so no problem there, thank goodness.'

Kate knew what he meant. 'You're operating now, sir?'

- 'Yes, you can get her ready. Leave the final skin preparation to be done in theatre. Give the pre-medication intravenously . . . get a more rapid result. The husband has signed the consent form. I'll have her down at half-three.' He went out of the ward, nodding, as he did so, to one or two of his patients. He walked slowly as though he had all the time in the world. In the passage he spoke to Staff Nurse True, whom he scarcely recognised in brown cotton trousers and an orange over-blouse. Joan True was off duty, but had come to the ward to visit a friend who had been admitted for exploratory surgery.

The theatre porters came to fetch Mrs Romer soon after the start of visiting, when the ward was full of people, who watched the stretcher pass. There were awed comments and dramatic whispers—the loudest from Mrs Polden, who remarked to her sullen-faced, bovine daughter: 'You mark my words, now, Moll, she's got something wrong with her stummick, I've seen that look before . . . an ulcer, that's what she's got. You see if I'm not right. I'm not often wrong now, am I, Moll?' Her daughter shook her head. She wished she had got a waist like Sister's, she wished she was tall and slim, she wished her ma wouldn't rabbit on, telling her what to do; she looked at the clock and wished it was time to go.

Kate went with Mrs Romer to the anaesthetic room,

then came swiftly up again. She wanted to make sure that Mrs Flow, the new patient, was settling in. It was when she was leaving the row of lifts and crossing Penhallow landing that she got the first warning prickle that something was very wrong. The feeling increased, became urgent, clanging like bells in her brain. What was it . . . what had happened? Something had happened . . . something was very wrong!

Through the portholes of the corridor doors just before she punched them inwards, she could see a cluster of nurses in the passage near the side-wards. Nurse Heston came out of Miss Elder's room, she turned round and saw Kate coming. 'Oh, Sister!' Her face looked white and shocked.

'What is it? What's happened?' Kate demanded.

'It's Miss Elder . . . she's fallen! Someone forgot . . .'

'Let me through!' She all but pushed Nurse Heston aside, as she stumbled into the room. Her eyes took in the scene in one sweep . . . empty bed, clothes hanging loose, one cotside in the down position, Miss Elder on the floor, semi-prone, moaning and trying to rise. 'Miss Elder, it's Sister.' Kate dropped to her knees. 'Try to lie perfectly still.'

'My arm . . . my arm . . .'

'I know . . . I know!' She dragged the bedclothes free and covered Miss Elder, then felt for her pulse and looked sharply up at Nurse Heston. 'Fill hot bottles, pack them round her—Nurse Finn, get the Casualty Doctor. You've not tried to move her?' she asked Nurse Solly who, whey-faced, shook her head. 'Was it you who found her?'

'Yes, Sister.'

Questions chased in Kate's head. Why hadn't the cotside been in position? Who had left it hanging? Every member of the staff knew that, just after lunch, Miss

Elder's mind had wandered. She had thought she was in her own home, had thought the phone was ringing. She had wanted to get out several times, and it hadn't been easy to soothe her. Ian Casson's request of a week ago that cotsides be used had been so right . . . so perfectly right . . .

What was he going to say?

'Mr Casson must be told at once.' Kate packed the first of the bottles around Miss Elder as Nurse Heston brought them in.

'Shall I ring him?'

'Get him bleeped, it's his time for coming. Nurse Solly, fill two more bottles.' Was Miss Elder hurt . . . badly hurt . . . had she broken her arm? Had she other injuries . . . would she be all right? How could it have happened? How could it have happened? Kate's mind continued to whirl.

As she knelt there, holding Miss Elder's hand, she heard approaching footsteps and a mutter of voices, which she couldn't distinguish. Two men were coming in . . . Ian, followed by Dr Formby. 'Now, what have you been doing, my dear little lady?' Harold Formby squatted down.

'How?' was the mute question written on Ian's face.

'She fell out of bed.'

He still didn't speak, just pushed in front of Kate. Dr Formby was quick, his hands going expertly over Miss Elder's body. She felt nothing till they rolled her over, when the pain leapt in her arm. Ian supported it, Kate saw him and Dr Formby exchange glances. 'We're going to get you back into bed.' They lifted her up like a baby, placing her in a half-sitting position; Kate fetched extra pillows. 'And a sling, please, Sister. Oh, good, you've brought one,' Harold Formby nodded approval. Kate fixed the sling, the bed was remade, the cotside hitched in place, then she and the two men adjourned to the office next door.

'I'll send one of the orthopaedic team up, get an X-ray done, but she's fractured both radius and ulna, I'd stake my life on that.' Harold Formby cocked an eye at Kate.

'Looks that way.' Ian paced the floor, one grey-suited leg coming out smartly in front of the other, shoulders slightly hunched Kate sensed his tension, felt it as though it were her own; it was a tension that denoted anger, she observed the line of his jaw. 'The very *last* thing I wanted to happen!' His voice was dangerously quiet.

'I'm not surprised.' Dr Formby's tone, in contrast, was easy and light. 'It means another GA, internal fixation of bones, long-arm plaster for eight or ten weeks . . . very bad luck all round.'

Two hours later, with the diagnosis confirmed by X-ray film, Miss Elder was taken down to the ortho-paedic theatre complex. Mrs Romer, the appen-dicectomy, was returned to the ward. William Jarman had been right, her appendix had ruptured and peritoni-tis had followed; a suprapubic drain was in situ, and she would have to be carefully nursed in a sitting position; she was very ill indeed.

Kate stayed on duty. With so much happening, she felt she couldn't leave. And somehow or other she had to make time to question all her staff. She had to find out—for she knew that Ian would demand an expla-nation—who had left Miss Elder's cotside down. It wasn't a task she relished, but she knew it was up to her to find out who could have been so negligent. So she interviewed every one of them, including Zia. The latter took umbrage, insisting that she had nothing to do with beds. 'If I ever took her a drink in, I handed it over her rails.' Nurses Solly and Finn and Heston had each taken the rails down that day . . . for bedmaking, for pressure point rubbing, and for dressing her ear, but they were all sure they had notched the sides up securely afterwards.

'Well, someone must have been to blame . . . she couldn't undo them herself!' Kate was tired, she sounded impatient, and disbelieving as well. Zia flushed with temper.

'It could have been you . . . you were in and out seeing how she was! It could have been you . . . you're no different from us . . . you're staff, the same as us!'

'Thank you, Zia. I've already asked myself the same kind of questions that I've put to you. I'm aware of my own involvement in it all.' Zia deserved to be told off, but the last thing Kate wanted was an upstanding row with any of them; she needed their support. Yet someone was lying, they had to be . . . *someone* had been careless. 'You may go,' she said curtly to Zia, and the girl flounced off. She was late already, and her boyfriend was in the yard.

The anaesthetist arrived to see Mrs Flow, due for tonsillectomy the following day, and Kate went with him while he asked the usual questions and made an examination of Mrs Flow's chest. When she returned to the office Ian was there, looking with unseeing eyes through the viewing window into the ward. As she entered and closed the door behind her, the little click it made filled her head, and the room, with sound; she spoke before he could utter. 'How is Miss Elder?' She knew he had been in theatre, keeping an eye on his patient, perhaps assisting while the broken arm was fixed.

He turned and looked at her, chin high, his words sailing over her head. 'She's come through it, and is down in Martindale, the orthopaedic ward. The arm will need to be elevated for the next two days.'

'But she'll come back here after then, won't she?'
Kate's voice was hoarse. She was nervous. She expected
a showdown—that was why he was here. He had come
to ask questions about the accident, he would want an
explanation.

'I don't know about that.' He felt low, depressed. He
dropped down into a chair. 'I'm forced to think it might
be best to leave her where she is.'

'But *why*?' She knew why, or could guess why, but
she couldn't let it rest, she couldn't let his remark go
unchallenged, he must come out and say what he
meant.

'Well, since you ask, I'll tell you.' One quick movement brought him to his feet in front of her. 'I feel that
what happened to Caroline Elder was the result of
carelessness on the part of your staff, for whose actions
you are to blame!' Kate moved to protest, but he held up
his hands. 'All right, you're busy, I know. You're short-
staffed, with too many patients, but that should make
you careful . . . extra careful to keep tabs on your
nurses, extra diligent!'

'I do my best.' Her retort was followed by a small, cold
silence . . . a silence that was every bit as chastening as if
he had filled it up with the bald statement that her best
wasn't good enough.

'I would even go farther,' he continued smoothly,
turning away from her. 'You were against cotsides,
weren't you? You didn't want them used.' He began to
walk up and down the small room, his movements fussed
and confused her.

'That's simply not true!'

'I think it *is*!' He stopped pacing and faced her close
to. 'Oh, I don't mean that you didn't do as I asked. You
gave the instruction no doubt. But perhaps you didn't
lend it much weight, emphasise its importance, give it

much credence . . . you treated it as a joke!'

'I certainly didn't!' she protested.

'As a whim, then!'

'No!'

'That kind of attitude shows,' he told her stiffly.

'But you're wrong . . . you're so wrong . . . there was no question! You just couldn't be more wrong. I upheld you, made your wishes plain, made those wishes mine. I agree that someone's been careless, someone has let us . . . *me* down. I've questioned everyone, every nurse on duty, and they all say the same thing . . . that they never, at any time, left her bed unrailed.'

'Then someone's lying!'

Kate looked at the floor; the same thought had occurred to her. After all, what else could she think? Someone was afraid . . . was afraid to own up, and that self-same person must now be praying hard that Miss Elder was too confused at the time to remember anything. 'I think you're being very unfair,' her voice grated harshly. In much the same way as she had defended *him* to the nurses, so must she defend them to him. Loyalty worked both ways . . . or was it divided? She bit her lip and her eyes reflected her wretchedness. 'You're unfair,' she said again, and watched him turn round from the window, head and shoulders outlined against the sky.

'Unfair!' he exploded. 'Unfair, Sister! I'll tell you what's unfair! What's unfair in *my* eyes is that a patient under your care, already confused by being in hospital, and by aural surgery, has had to have a second anaesthetic, and a second surgery procedure, all because someone . . . someone *up here* . . . has been bloody negligent!'

'I can only say how sorry I am,' Kate managed to say at last. And she *was* sorry, deeply so, but the anger in her voice at the sheer injustice of most of the things he had thrown at her head was a poor conveyor of words of apology.

A delicate coughing sound in the doorway—neither had heard the door open—stopped any further heated exchange; William Jarman came into the room. 'If I might interrupt,' he said to Ian, 'I would like a word with Sister . . . in the ward, if you please, my dear. I need your expert advice. Sorry to take her from you, old man, but she does belong to me . . . well, so to speak. I can't do without her for long.' This, and the fatherly smile he gave her, and the pat in the small of her back, made it plain to Kate that William Jarman had heard part of their argument and was doing his best to revive her confidence. It was good of him, but she wasn't grateful. She liked to fight her own battles.

'Excuse me,' she said to Ian, 'and again, I apologise.' Then she followed Mr Jarman out of the room.

In the ward he gave her instructions about the peritonitis case, and also about Mrs Polden on whom he wished to operate in four days' time. 'We've waited long enough. As for you, Sister, you've done wonders to slim her as much as you have.' He was singing her praises, and the sound was balm. Mr Jarman approved of her; she felt a shade less fretted when she went off duty at last.

She was surprised to meet Olly on the landing. Denuded of his overall, he looked even more bulky in light fawn trousers and a check sports jacket which strained at the front and rucked up under his arms. 'You're late, Kathryn,' he whisked over to her with his quick, light tread.

'You are too.'

'Chapter of accidents,' he explained.

You and I both, she thought, standing beside him as

the lift took them down three floors. The revolving glass doors in the main hall showed a rainy scene outside.

'Terrible weather, more like April.' Olly took her arm. 'Come and have a coffee and a plate of sandwiches over at the Creamery, Kathryn. I've something to tell you.' His face looked woebegone.

Rather to her surprise, Kate heard herself accept. She could tell Olly what had happened, she could tell him anything. He was that sort . . . a good listener; he would tell her what he thought, but be comforting too, and he wouldn't inwardly gloat.

Over mugs of coffee and a pile of crab sandwiches —Olly was ravenous—he told her his own, very sad item of news: 'Carl Johns, the lorry driver who plunged into the ENT Clinic, died, Kathryn . . . early this afternoon.'

Kate stared at him. She knew Carl Johns had been in Fratton Ward, and getting on so very well, according to all reports. 'But I thought he was getting on, Olly, I thought he would be all right!'

'So did we all . . . so did we all,' Olly shook his head. 'He had a cerebral haemorrhage on the way back from the bathrooms, just fell down and died; there was nothing we could do.'

'After all this time? Oh, I'm *so* sorry!'

'It's five weeks now, nearly six, but William Jarman suspected that he might have had some sort of seizure, when he had the accident. Carl himself said he seemed to black out, but nothing very significant showed up on the electro-encephalogram.'

'I'm sorry,' Kate said again.

'Jarman was upset, so was Casson—he took an interest, used to chat to him. A death on the ward runs right through it, affects the staff *and* patients. As for his girl-friend, poor little thing, she couldn't take it in. I've been talking to her, that's really why I'm late.' Olly's appetite was the nervous sort, he took another sandwich. As he bit into it, easing his stress, Kate told him about Miss Elder and the row with Ian, but she tried to play it down.

'Well, of course,' Olly said ruminatively, 'he was upset over Carl, which might account for some of the anger he vented on you. And I know what you mean when you say you feel let down by your staff, or by one member of it . . . not a pleasant feeling at all. I've had it happen to me once or twice in the past. Incidentally, you'll have to write a report for Miss Rone, you know. Everything like that has to go through all the proper channels, just in case the patient decides to sue.'

'I'm writing the report at home tonight. Do you think she'll sue?'

'No . . . no, course not,' Olly wobbled his chins. 'Take it a step at a time, Kathryn, and always bear in mind that no one is perfect, and from what I've been hearing, you're a good Ward Sister. No one could possibly blame you for what has occurred.'

Someone already has, Kate thought, but she didn't go on about it. It was six-thirty, and she ought to be getting home. Outside the rain streamed down, there were far-off rumbles of thunder, and summer lightning, like a great big blink in the sky.

'You can't go now, you'll get soaked,' said Olly. He couldn't bear getting wet.

'I shall have to risk it.' Kate got to her feet. 'Thanks for the coffee, Olly.' Leaving him try to choose between a meringue and a mille-feuille slice, she pushed through the tables and made her way to the doors.

Exactly opposite the Creamery Rooms was the stately

City Hall, next to that was the Public Library, and
coming down its steps, all but hidden by a many-hued
golfing umbrella, was Ellis. Kate stood at the kerb and
waved. He hurried across, dodging the traffic; he
reached her and held the umbrella over them both, as
the rain drove at it like stones.

'A chance meeting, but nicely timed!' Kate said above
the din.

Ellis smiled in his cautious fashion; there were papers
under his arm. 'I saw you go into the café,' he said. 'I've
been in the Reference Library, till they turned me out,
they're closing now . . . but aren't you unusually
late?'

'Very.' She didn't explain. 'Would you like a lift? The
Fiat's just round the corner from here, in the hospital
park.'

'I would, thank you. I came in by bus, due to the
parking problem. It's a very congested area.'

'You can say that again! Anyway, be my guest!' In
no time at all they had rounded the corner and were
climbing into her car.

There was no sign of Ian's Rover in the hospital park.
Kate's eyes took in the marked-out oblong of deserted
wet tarmac, as she and Ellis drove out of the exit gates.
He had probably gone some time ago. Her mind jerked
and flicked in rhythm with the windscreen wipers which
were forcing her to remember, daring her to forget the
things he had said . . . 'you are to blame' . . . 'tabs on
your nurses' . . . 'bloody negligent'. She burned with
anger, cooled with uncertainty. Could he have been
right? Was she strong enough with her staff? Did she
check up enough? If anything I oversee them too much,
she thought, as she rolled her window down. I check
and re-check, and I sometimes annoy them, especially
Staff Nurse True. And it's no good going over and over

it—at least not now. I'll think about it when I get home, I've got to write that report—the report that will have to go in to the SNO.

The first set of traffic lights, in the lee of the great Cathedral, were turning red as Kate approached them, and as she waited there a pale car drew up alongside, heading the second lane. Even before she turned her head she guessed what she would see—a white Rover, and behind its wheel a man with thick fair hair, cleanly-cut features, a forceful thrust to his jaw. She was right on all counts; there he sat, immovable as stone . . . till he turned and saw her, and Ellis beside her; he nodded politely to both.

'Wasn't that the fellow from the hospital who brought you home that day when you cracked your head?' Ellis watched the car speed away on the green. Kate was slower, and pips sounded from behind.

'Yes, that's right.'

'He's a slippy driver.' The Rover was out of sight, swallowed up in the traffic flowing east.

When they got home Ellis asked Kate if she would share his evening meal. The invitation didn't surprise her, for knowing him as she now did, she guessed he would feel obliged to make some return for the lift. She also guessed—as it happened, rightly—that he wanted her to refuse. He wanted to work, she needed to be on her own for the rest of the evening. 'Thank you, Ellis, but no,' she said. 'I've one or two things I must do.'

'Another time, then.' He was glad to get out and stretch his legs free of cramps. The rain had ceased and a thin sun was streaking the clouds with silver.

'I would like that.' She was smiling as she ran the car into the garage. That was the best thing about an easy, uncomplicated relationship. Neither side could be hurt by the other, there were no peaks of feeling.

It was rather like sailing on a calm, untroubled sea.

CHAPTER SEVEN

MISS RONE sent for Kate at ten-thirty next morning. She had read her report of the accident, and had been to see Miss Elder in Martindale Ward. Kate, who was expecting the summons, went down to Admin Block, breathing deeply to quell her nervousness.

Angela Rone didn't miss the look of strain on the thin young face. Was she pushing the girl too hard? Had it been fair to burden her—*over*burden her, with extra patients, so soon after coming here?

'What has happened is unfortunate, Kathryn. You won't need me to tell you that,' she said, towards the end of their talk. She had taken infinite pains to soft-pedal the laying of any blame. 'You're not shielding any of your nurses, are you?' Her eyes were needle-sharp. 'Because that would be extremely foolish, both for their sake and yours.'

'No, Miss Rone. I've questioned them all. I don't even have any suspicions. I just can't tell you how sorry I am that such a thing could have happened.'

'All right, Sister. We'll just have to hope that the poor woman gets on well. I'm sure she will,' Miss Rone added, allowing herself to smile. Kate left her office, not feeling a great deal better. Oh, if only the mystery could be solved!

When she got back to Penhallow Ward Ian's patient, Mrs Flow, was being wheeled down to theatres for her tonsillectomy. 'Another one for the chop, eh?' Mrs Polden came out of the kitchen. She hadn't bargained on running full tilt into Kate in the corridor. 'No, Sister, I

haven't been eating, there was nothing lying about . . .
not that I would have touched it, not with me operation
coming up the day after tomorrow, on Friday the thir-
teenth. You don't think that means I'll die, do you?
Could it be a sign . . . you don't think so, do you,
Sister?' Kate saw the alarm in her eyes.

'No, Mrs Polden, I certainly don't. You're going to be
all right. Now, come back to bed, and we'll talk about it.'
She took the woman's arm. Mrs Polden, for all her
cocksureness, for all her I-know-best ways, was nervous,
and needed reassurance. She leaned heavily on Kate;
there was so much to harry her just at this time.

The morning wore on. William Jarman did his round,
accompanied by Derek Coles. Mrs Romer, the peritonitis case, was already responding to drugs. Her tem-
perature was down, her pulse less rapid, her breathing
easier. 'She's going to do.' William Jarman was pleased,
as he walked to the ward desk with Kate. 'When I
opened her up I got a shock . . . good thing we got to her
fast! Right, then, Sister, let's get on,' and he led the way
to the next bed, Kate and the houseman following in his
wake.

Mrs Flow came back from theatre, and was transferred to her bed in the tonsillectomy position—lying on
her right side, right leg drawn up to form a ledge. Kate
left Nurse Solly to sit with her. 'She must lie in that
position until she wakes up, and when she does, call me
at once.' She went out of the side-ward, leaving the door
ajar.

She found time, during her lunch break, to go to see
Miss Elder. She was making her way down Martindale
corridor when she ran into Ian. He was coming away
from the ward, looking thoughtful and oppressed. When
he saw her he jarred to a halt and blinked, as though she
had broken his trance. 'If you're going along to see Miss

Elder, she's fast asleep,' he said.

'I won't wake her, but if Sister will let me, I would like to see how she is.' If she didn't go forward into the ward, she would have to turn back with him, and she didn't want to do that; she wasn't prepared enough. She hadn't recovered from yesterday, from those stinging things he had said. It would take another day at least before she could square up to him and look him in the eye without a twitch.

'As you like,' she heard him say, and his face was inscrutable, as he turned it towards the landing doors.

Miss Elder's plastered arm looked like a white branch of a tree. It was drawn out at right angles to her body, and suspended by bandages to the beam of a Balkan frame beside her bed. She was raised high on her pillows; she looked peaceful, and pretty, and pink, and as Ian had said, deep in the realms of sleep. Kate looked at her and went away; there was no point in staying. All the nurses were busy and Sister was at lunch. She decided she would do the same, and feeling very slightly better, she joined Olly in the cafeteria.

She was on lates next day, and going on duty just before one o'clock, she saw to her great delight that Miss Elder was back in the side-ward. The pleasure appeared to be mutual, for Miss Elder was all smiles. 'They were good to me in Orthopaedics, Sister, but this is my proper place, even with those.' Cotsides were up at her bed.

'You may not need them after today. We're playing safe, Miss Elder.'

Kate turned with a start to see Ian standing close behind her. 'Sorry to make you jump, Sister. I've been stealing a bite from your kitchen, rather like Mrs Polden, but I missed lunch today.'

'Tough!' was on the tip of Kate's tongue. 'I hope Zia

looked after you,' were her actual and very proper words.

'Thank you, yes.'

They left Miss Elder and went into the office. 'I'm so glad she's back!' Kate couldn't keep the relief and pleasure she felt out of her voice. For I'm glad, she added silently, deep within herself, I'm glad she's back because you've shown, by allowing her to do so, that you feel she's safe in my keeping . . . in a way it's a gesture of faith. And thank you, Ian, at any rate for that.

'I had no choice,' was his crushing reply, 'they had an accident case brought into Orthopaedics this morning, and Miss Elder's bed was wanted.'

'I'm still glad to have her, whatever the reason!' Kate replied just as crushingly.

He looked at her, noted the flash in her eye, the way she stood her ground, arms straight, fingers curled into their palms. 'Let's get on, shall we?' he said more amenably. 'I would like to see Mrs Flow and Mrs Bealer, please.'

He always said 'please', but sometimes he said it in a very annoying way. She was glad to turn her back to reach for the notes.

Mrs Polden had her gall-bladder operation the following morning. All went well, despite the 'unlucky' date. On Saturday Mrs Bealer was discharged, entirely free of pain. She kept thanking Kate over and over again for all that she had done. 'I've not felt as well as this for a couple of years,' she declared.

'It was Mr Casson who cured you,' said Kate.

'Yes, I know, but you got me through. You've been a real friend.' Mrs Bealer's hand, still a little clammy from weakness, grasped Kate's, and she thanked her all over again.

'Don't forget your outpatients appointment, and keep

in close touch with your doctor,' Kate told her, saying goodbye to both her and her husband. The lift arrived and Mrs Bealer was gone.

'A satisfied customer!' Ian was crossing the landing. He had said his farewells to the Bealers earlier on.

'We do have them . . . occasionally,' Kate assured him.

'All the time, I'm sure.'

What was he being, Kate wondered, patronising or pleasant, and if the latter, had Mr Jarman been having a word with him? He was hovering, standing right in her path, so what was she meant to do? If she did what she really wanted, she would say 'excuse me' and go, push past him, if necessary, get back on to the ward. She could have done that . . . oh, so easily . . . to Ian the man, but not to Casson the surgeon, there was such a thing as protocol, so she stood her ground, looking up at him.

'Did you want something, sir?'

There was just a second when he seemed to incline towards her, there was a single in-the-balance second when he seemed about to say something which might have resolved the coolness between them, made things less difficult, but the second passed, and nothing was said. He moved away from her. 'Not a single thing,' and he joined the small crowd at the lifts.

At lunch Olly was waiting for Kate, beaming from ear to ear. She hardly had time to sit down before he began to pour out his good news. 'You and I have been *chosen*, Kathryn—Miss Rone has just told me, she'll be seeing you later this afternoon. It's quite an honour in its way, but I think it's well deserved.'

Kate didn't ask what he was talking about, she knew he would come to that, once his fizzle of glee had run its course. 'We've been chosen,' he explained, 'to receive the guests at the consultants' cocktail party, to be held in the boardroom on the twenty-seventh of July.'

'What?' she gasped, fork in mid-air. 'You have to be joking, Olly!'

'They have this party every year—consultants only invited,' he told her. 'They come from all over the Duchy of Cornwall, from five other hospitals. It's hosted by the Administrator and Miss Rone, as SNO, but they always have two senior staff to receive the guests at the main doors and direct them through.'

'Ushers, you mean?'

'Rather more than that,' Olly looked reproving. 'We're allowed to go in and join them, once they've all arrived.'

'Big deal!'

'That's exactly what it is, not so much a deal as an honour. One meets some very eminent men, and ladies too, of course. There are one or two lady consultants. The men aren't allowed to bring wives . . . it's a strictly professional gathering . . . and you and I have been asked.'

Kate's shepherd's pie cooled on its plate as she stared at it unseeingly. The import of Olly's words was sinking in. 'But why us? Why me? I've only just come here!' she protested.

'It's because we've been helping out so magnificently with extra patients, Kathryn. We've done well, worked wonders, there's no denying that.'

'You have, I don't know about me.' She thought of Miss Elder again, and all the resulting suspicion and unpleasantness. Nothing had been quite the same between her and her nurses since. And as for Ian . . . as for him . . . well, of course, he would be at the party. 'I shan't go,' she said. 'I shall tell Miss Rone I'm too new.'

'But you can't do that!' Olly was aghast. 'She won't

ask you, anyway, she'll tell you . . . it's like a royal command. Unless you're ill you can't refuse, you can't get out of it. Come, my dear, you can do it with me,' a plump hand patted Kate's, 'we'll make a splendid couple, the best they've ever had.' Olly thought happily of the new dark suit he had just had made for him. With it he would wear a nice bright tie and one of his pure silk shirts. 'It's a chance to dress up—we don't wear uniform. Get out your prettiest dress; we'll show them what's what! Now, no more talk of saying no.'

Kate finished her lunch, scarcely aware of what she put in her mouth. A party, in the boardroom on Friday week . . . she had nothing she could wear, nothing really suitable, she had one after-six dress, but she had lost weight since she had been in Cornwall and it would hang on her like a sack, unless it was altered, and she wasn't exactly a wizard at needlework. I suppose I could buy a new one, she thought; it might be fun to dress up. As she sat there thinking about it while Olly ate his pudding, the first little nip of determination and, yes, of excitement too, began to strengthen Kate's resolve, push her towards a decision, spur her on; her green hazel eyes had a glint. She would go to that party, pull all the stops out, buy a new dress and shoes, spare no expense to make herself ravishing. 'Okay, Olly,' she said at last, 'when our esteemed SNO issues her invitation, or royal command, I'll smile and be grateful . . . curtsey and say yes, please.'

In the end Evelyn Sawyer helped her buy her dress. Kate arranged to meet her on her next days off, and was invited to Eve's flat over Asterfords, the big department store. They lunched in the flat, then took the lift down into the Store proper. There they made their way to Fashions, where Eve sought out the buyer, a hawk-faced woman with jet hair and a cool assessing eye. 'Green, rose, or cream with your colouring,' she said. Ushering them into a fitting-room, she brought in several dresses. Kate tried on four, but the moment she saw the cream flocked lace, she knew it was hers . . . it had to be hers; she slid it over her head, put her arms in the sleeves, let the black-haired buyer zip her up at the back, felt the whispering, silky touch of the skirt flowing about her hips. It was midi-length, and the hem had a scalloped edge. 'It's perfect with your hair and skin!' Eve pirouetted round her. 'But you'll need earrings, Kate, long ones, and pointed stiletto shoes.'

'I've got some earrings, carved ivory ones; they'll do very well,' said Kate, prudence doing battle with her mood of recklessness. 'But shoes, yes, I'll get new ones—gold ones, I think. They'll pick up the gold link belt of the dress.'

'Madam has good taste,' the buyer said, unzipping her again.

The dress was packed, the shoes were bought, and after saying 'hello' to Eve's colleagues on the beauty counter, the two girls repaired to the third-floor restaurant for tea. The tea-room was large and not very crowded at such an early hour, which was how they saw—could hardly miss—the couple at the far end: Ian and Helen Reever. 'Look!' Eve's face lit up.

'I've already looked, and if you stare you'll have *them* looking too.'

'They're coming over, or one of them is . . . the girl, I rather think.' Eve was sitting facing them. 'I wonder what she wants.'

Helen, in skin-tight pants and a top that showed every line and curve, wanted advice on a new range of make-up; it was Eve she wanted to see. 'Ian told me who you were,' she said, 'and I've seen you on your counter; I looked for you there this afternoon.' She smiled absently at Kate.

'I'm not back at work till next week,' said Eve, 'but I'll show you the range, if you like. I'm sure my girls would help you, though.' Their tea had just arrived, and Kate was putting milk into the cups.

'I would rather *you* showed me, if you possibly could. Is that asking too much? The thing is I've got to be back at my shop in under half an hour.' No one could look more appealing than Helen when she gave her mind to it. Eve smiled resignedly, pushing back her chair.

'All right, Miss Reever, I'll come down with you. Start tea, Kate, and wait for me here. I shouldn't be very long.'

Kate watched them go. Helen Reever, she reflected, had an over-abundance of cheek! She poured her tea, and after an obligatory smile in Ian's direction, began to drink it, facing front, trying to forget his presence. She found this difficult, especially when, after a minute or two, he crossed the room and stood at her table. 'May I?' he looked at Eve's chair.

'Please do.' Kate set down her cup; she knew her hand wasn't steady. Please don't let him see I'm nervous . . . please don't let him guess how he affects me. 'What a lovely afternoon!' she added brightly.

'Perfect.' He arranged himself on the chair opposite, avoiding her parcels against the table leg. 'Our friends are off painting the lily, I take it?'

'Yes, but they won't be long. Eve is an expert painter of lilies, she'll give Helen good advice. Perhaps you would like her cup of tea?' she pushed it towards his hand. 'I can soon get another when she returns.'

'Thank you.' He dropped in three lumps of sugar, seeming to have to concentrate over-hard as he put the tongs back in the bowl. 'You're on days off, are you?' He glanced at her swiftly, then back again at his cup.

'Until Thursday, yes.'

'You need them, I'm sure.'

'A break makes all the difference.'

'I don't doubt it.' His lashes lay unmoving on his cheeks, lavishly thick, fair lashes, lightly tanned cheeks . . . medical men seldom have time to get brown.

'Eve and I have been shopping.' Dear heaven, how awful this was, straining for words across the table, the very air above it solid and hard like the skin of a tightly stretched drum.

'Asterfords is good for most things.' Ian looked at the plan on the wall just beside them; it showed the store layout, and Kate looked at it too. 'They have a good photographic department,' his finger pointed it out, 'and I'm looking for a new camera, so I may go and see what they've got.' He began to enlarge on the subject of cameras, which Kate knew nothing about. He was still talking, and she was listening, when Eve and Helen returned. It was difficult to say who was the more relieved to be interrupted. Ian sprang to his feet and shook hands with Eve; Helen dangled an Asterfords bag, a smaller edition of the long boxed one that lay on the floor beside Kate. 'I must go, darling,' she put a small fuchsia-tipped hand on his arm, 'I'm late as it is. Are you coming, or stopping?'

'Coming, of course!' he said so quickly that even Eve looked surprised.

'She's got him exactly where she wants him,' she commented as the two made off.

'Unless he wants to be there too, I doubt it very much. He's not the sort to be tugged about willy-nilly, Eve. He wanted to go just now, so he went. Helen rescued him.'

'That's a funny way of putting it.' Eve gave Kate a searching look. 'All I can say is, it didn't take him long to make a beeline for you. He must have come over as soon as my back was turned.'

'He's never rude, he could hardly ignore me,' protested Kate.

'No, maybe not.' Even tested the teapot to see how full it was. 'Let's have some more, this has got cold.' She signalled to the waitress, who came at once. Eve was well-known in the Store. 'That girl bought masses of stuff,' she confided, as the two of them settled down with their fresh pot of tea, and Kate did her best to relax. 'She doesn't look as though she needs a thing, but who am I to dissuade her from spending a mint in my department?'

'She's got plenty of money to spend,' Kate told her.

'*Has* she?'

'Well, so I hear.'

'Bully for her! Mr Casson looked rather pained; perhaps he disapproves of all her wild extravagance.'

It's me he disapproves of, thought Kate, but she didn't say so out loud. 'He's not an easy man, you know, Eve. It was *awkward* talking to him.'

'You mean when you're not at the hospital?'

'Yes, I suppose I mean that.' There was far more *to* it than that, but she couldn't explain to Eve. An innate reserve prevented her from telling her new-found friend how Ian affected her, how she felt about him, how she wished him to think her competent, how she wanted to be able to work with him in peace. Anything else was out, for she herself had made that clear. And thank goodness she had; he was bound up with, entrenched with Helen Reever. Most likely they would marry—they had looked married crossing the restaurant together, he carrying her dangling parcels, bending to hear what she said, she small, as high as his heart . . . there I go again, twisting myself into futile, stupid knots, thought Kate.

'I think he fancies you,' said Eve, bringing Kate's

thought meanderings back into the hard, straight line of shock.

'Don't be silly, Eve!' she protested.

'Will he be at the party?'

'Yes, I think he will, he's bound to be, he's the right status, and everything.'

'Well, whoever it is you want to wow, you'll succeed in that gem of a dress . . . wish I could be there, a fly on the wall, just to see what gives.'

'Impossible!' Kate couldn't help laughing. Eve was good for the ego. Even the most independent of humans need encouragement at times, need moral support, a bit of a boost, their talents recognised. Eve was supplying all these aids, and one more was to come.

'Let me do your face and nails on the night of the party,' she said. 'I *am* a trained beautician, you know, and I'd do it very cheapo . . . just for the price of a lift to your cottage and back.'

'I've never had a professional make-up,' said Kate.

'I could make you look gorgeous Kate, and with very little artifice too, just a touch here and there.' Eve looked at her with her eyes half-closed, as though getting her in perspective.

'Stop the survey, and get on with your tea. Your offer is accepted, Madame Beautician!' smiled Kate, giving in.

CHAPTER EIGHT

A week passed, a week and two days, and Friday the twenty-seventh, the day of the consultants' party, arrived. It was the day, too, when Miss Elder went home with her arm in plaster, and a card for Outpatients' Clinic in her bag. 'It's a relief to have my dizziness cured, the arm is nothing, Sister,' she said, shaking hands with her left hand, and going off with her mother, who was eighty-eight, had good hearing and, as she told Kate on the side, had never suffered with dizziness in her life.

Mrs Flow, the tonsillectomy, had gone out a week ago, which left Kate—for the first time since the ENT Clinic disaster—with no patient of Ian's in her ward.

'So unless he sends us someone else, he won't be gracing us with his presence again,' said Nurse True, watching Nurse Solly stripping Miss Elder's bed.

'True enough,' Kate replied, 'but perhaps we're due for a rest.'

'Fat chance of that with twenty-eight patients of Mr Jarman's in the main ward. Still, let's count our blessings.' Joan True looked at her watch. 'In another two hours our Mrs Polden will be getting into her taxi. And I'm sorry, Sister, but I can't say I'm sorry; since she's been feeling better, she's bounced up again like a rubber ball, telling us all what to do. Why, she even gave William Jarman advice about keeping his weight down, and that coming from her was really rich!'

'Whatever did he say?' Kate couldn't help smiling. Dear Mr Jarman was pear-shaped!

'Said he'd bear her comments in mind—he was

kindness itself to her. He even said he would try to get up to the ward to bid her goodbye. He really is a decent sort, he never goes up in the air. You can't ruffle him . . . you never see him mad.'

'No,' said Kate . . . unlike some, she added under her breath. She had seen Ian yesterday, and he had been politeness itself, but with the same cool aura eddying about him, as though he moved in a capsule of chilly air. She was certain he wouldn't be in a hurry to send more patients into Penhallow. He wouldn't entrust them into her nursing care.

True to his word, Mr Jarman appeared as Mrs Polden was leaving on the arm of her stolid and glowering son. She hailed William with obvious relief. 'Wait here,' she instructed her son. Then she took Kate's arm. 'I want a word with both of you in private.'

'In private?' William Jarman looked startled.

'Here will be all right.' She shunted them into a small alcove just to the right of the lifts. 'I want to clear meself, you see, before I leave 'ere for good.'

'Clear yourself? But my dear lady . . .'

'Not me stones, sir, I know they're gorn, it's me conscience,' she touched her chest. 'It was me who took that rail down from Carrie Elder's bed. She was upset, see . . . didn't like the rails. I'd heard her going on about them all that morning, so I laid low, and waited me chance. I went in there during the quiet time, she was asleep, but I still did it. I thought it'd give her a chance to show she was okay without 'em. But then I heard she'd fell out, and I felt bad about it, but me own op was coming up, and I didn't dare say a word all the time I was feeling so ill, in case you turned me out, or give me a rotten time, like . . .'

'Mrs *Polden*!' Kate was appalled. Just for a second she forgot the 'crime' and thought only of the reason Mrs

Polden had given for feeling she ought to keep quiet.

'It was a very wrong thing to do!' William Jarman went brick red.

'I know that now, sir.'

'And other people got the blame for it. All this time Sister has been most worried, most unhappy about the position, not to mention Miss Elder herself.'

'Going home plastered, you mean?' Conscience appeased, Mrs Polden was regaining her confidence. 'I saw her before she went home, and I confessed to her as well. She said I was to talk to you, Sister, but I wanted to tell you, sir . . . tell you as well, you being my surgeon, the one who got me through all me agony. You had a right to know.'

'Miss Elder was Mr Casson's patient.' Kate was recovering her breath, and finding her voice; well really, she thought, well really, after all this time!

'You can tell him, then, can't you, dear?' Mrs Polden was backing away. 'I must go now—thanks a lot, it's nice to be going 'ome.' She and her son entered the lift, which had sailed up to level four; it sailed down, bearing them off, leaving Kate and William Jarman looking at one another, mouthing a mutual . . . *well*!

'I just never thought of a patient daring to do a thing like that. She knew how to get the rail down too. Was there anything she *didn't* know?' said Kate at last, speaking half to herself.

'You've not had a very easy passage since you've been here, have you, Sister?' William Jarman looked at her, envying her her youth. 'It's not often we get a patient as interfering as Mrs Polden, nor as lacking in common sense.'

'I'm glad it's all cleared up now. I'm more glad than I can say that it wasn't one of my ward team,' Kate said earnestly. 'All the same, sir, it's still down to me—I should have watched her more closely. I always thought it was the kitchen that lured her out of the ward. I ought to have seen, I should have cracked down on her more.'

'Not in your nature, my dear, I think. You're not the cracking down sort.' Patting her arm, smiling at her, looking more pear-shaped than ever, he climbed the stairs to the doctors' dining-room. There was no chance of seeing Casson there, he knew he lunched at the Clinic, but they would doubtless meet at the cocktail party tonight.

They did, both arriving late and conversing for several minutes before parting company and mingling with their peers. Kate and Olly, the receiving part of their duty long since done, were chatting to several people they knew. Kate, as Mr Drew, the ophthalmic surgeon, had just informed her, was a sight for sore eyes in her elegant dress, her burnished nut-brown hair coiled in a chignon low in the nape of her neck. Her face, discreetly made up by Eve, had a glow and liveliness that had been missing from it recently; Eve had an artist's touch. 'You look terrific, Kate,' she had said, and her words, or others similar, had been repeated many times tonight.

It was a relief, towards the end of the evening, to be back in Olly's company, and from his side, Kate surveyed the scene. There were sixty medical men at least, all of consultant rank, standing around in over-large groups, laughing and cracking jokes, some of them blue, as well as talking shop. The women were hopelessly outnumbered, Kate counted five. Ian was talking to one of them—a wandy lady in glasses, who Olly said was an ENT surgeon from Pailey Infirmary. Ian had been one of the last to arrive, Olly had shown him in. Kate, at that time, had been caught up with a black-bearded urologist from the Royal Queen's Hospital at Penzance.

The boardroom was large, but not quite large enough

to accommodate so many people. Some had spilled out of the open doors on to a colonnade which sheltered the front of Admin Block from the worst of the westerly gales. There was no gale this evening, not so much as a breeze; there was just the sunset, fiery and fierce, staining the sky vermilion and dying the fluted columns a pinkish cream.

Olly and Kate decided to move outside themselves, but almost immediately Olly was hailed by a robust man so very like himself in type that, viewed from behind, they looked like a matching pair, or identical twins. They even had the same fringed baldness, the same jug ears. Kate watched them idly, glad to be sitting down for a little while, glad not to have to be talking, but her respite was shortlived. She was joined within the next five minutes by the hirsute urologist, who asked her if he could get her something to drink. His teeth were white, his skin was swarthy, he looked like a dastardly pirate. All he needed was a cutlass, she thought, or a knife between his teeth. 'That's kind of you, but . . .' she started to say, just as a glass of wine appeared as if by magic under her nose. She grasped it, and turned, and there behind her chair was Ian; her pirate friend took his leave and Ian sat down.

'Neat, don't you think?' he smiled, but his eyes held a flicker of uncertainty. Perhaps Kate's did too, for why had he come, why the charade with the wine? 'I've been trying to speak to you ever since I came, but in the end, alas, I had to resort to desperate means.' It didn't escape his notice that she was setting her glass of wine down on a sill. 'Don't you like white wine?' he asked her. 'Can I get you something else?'

'I'm driving, so I'm abstaining,' she explained, hoping she didn't sound smug.

He nodded, but made no comment, and again Kate

wondered why he had bothered to seek her out like this. Their relationship over the past few weeks had been balanced on a knife-edge. Even a party atmosphere couldn't improve it immediately—not in one fell swoop, as Miss Rone would have said. Ian was turning his own glass of wine round and round on his knee. Kate stared at it, mesmerised. 'It's a super evening,' she said.

'Yes, just right for this sort of affair.'

'Were you invited last year?'

'Yes, I've been twice. I came to Cornwall in '82, you know.'

'Of course, I was forgetting.' She felt awkward, thinking of Rose.

'My wish to work in the West Country was one of the several things your sister and I disagreed about,' he told her.

'But I thought . . .' Kate stared.

'You thought I moved because of the fracas in London? You know, sometimes, Kate,' he smiled at her, 'things are not what they seem, neither are people.'

'No, I . . . I know. Rose never said very much.'

Ian ignored her remark, but commented quickly and fulsomely on her appearance. 'You look stunning, as I'm sure every red-blooded male in there must have told you.' He gestured towards the boardroom doors.

'I've not spoken to every red-blooded male yet!' She felt suddenly light and free, even joyous, but for goodness' sake, she castigated herself, don't read too much into a single compliment!

Several more groups were milling out on to the colonnade. Their chairs were surrounded, cigar and pipe smoke eddied above their heads. Ian flapped a hand in disgust. 'Let's get out of this, shall we? There's something I want to say to you, and I can't in all this din.'

'I agree, it's noisy.' They pushed their way through

and began to walk side by side, rather sedately along the arched colonnade. At first the ticking of Kate's narrow heels on the black and white-tiled floor was the only sound, then Ian cleared his throat.

'I want to apologise,' he began curtly. 'I saw Bill Jarman just now. He told me . . .'

'Please, don't go on.' They stopped walking and faced one another. 'Please don't go on, don't say any more, it's just not necessary.' Kate felt embarrassed, acutely so. She hadn't expected this. I've been wrong about him in many respects, she thought. I wish he wouldn't apologise. I'm still mainly to blame for what happened— Sisters always are, they're like punchballs, built to take the knocks.

'I've been feeling very disturbed about the whole thing,' he went on. 'I said some unforgivable things, made off-the-cuff accusations, which were so wide of the mark I wonder you didn't box my ears.'

'Sisters don't box consultants' ears, sir!' They both laughed at that, but uneasily and awkwardly. Kate tried to meet him halfway. 'Most of the blame attaches to me—I was angry and rude. I should have known about Mrs Polden's side-ward visits. Not everything you flung at me was unfair.'

'That's generous.' He touched her hair, traced the smudge of her bruise. 'It still shows, just faintly.' His face was near to hers.

'Eve tried her best to camouflage it.' She knew she ought to move . . . she ought to move . . . she ought to move back *now*.

'My grandmother had an infallible cure for bumps and bruises,' he told her, 'kiss and make better—I believe in it, most implicitly.' She felt his lips moving over her brow, his hands imprisoned her face, then he brought his mouth to hers in one swift, pressuring movement, a warm, hard, firm . . . then away, leaving her gasping and breathless, leaving her dizzy with happiness.

'Ian . . .' she began.

'The party's breaking up. We'd better go back, I think.' He touched her nose in a playful gesture. 'We'd better go, my Kate, before we break any more rules . . . *your* rules.' His eyes burned into hers.

'Let me drive you home—I've got the car. You've been drinking, you ought not to drive. Oh, I know not much,' she misread the slight shake of his head, 'you'll never get a taxi so late in the evening, unless you've got one ordered. It would be no trouble to me to run you home.'

It was terrible how her words dropped into silence, how he didn't answer her; it was useless and pointless to frantically want to snatch them back again. Coming along from the car-park end of the colonnade walk was a small figure in satin trousers, a sequin-spattered top, and high heels that clacked and clacked louder and louder and louder. Helen Reever . . . Helen, of course. Helen had come to fetch him. And who better? Helen was driving him home:

'Hi, Kate, long time no see! And my, don't you look gorgeous! Doesn't she, Ian? Jeepers, that dress!' For a girl who'd forsaken America, she wasn't averse to using its idioms.

'Hello, Helen.' Kate's greeting was drowned by the sound of car doors slamming, by the shouts of goodbyes as guests climbed into taxis or limousines—some of the latter driven by bored-looking wives. Olly was beckoning to her, she could see him from where she stood. 'Oh, heavens!' she turned about, 'I'm neglecting my social duties. I'm supposed to speed the departing guests, that was all part of the bargain; otherwise I might never have got in!'

The rest of the evening, the drive home, the snack meal she prepared and ate in the kitchen, passed in a haze of self-recrimination. How could I . . . how could I possibly have shown my hand like that? she asked herself. How *could* I have offered to drive him home, manoeuvred to be with him, alone with him, and shown him so plainly . . . yes, shown him that I wanted him? Because I *did* show him, and he wouldn't be slow to see everything I was thinking—everything that was passing through my mind.

Seeing Helen coming for him had been like a body blow, a blow to the heart . . . a little death. But why should I feel like that? Why should I feel as strongly as that? The answer reeled into her brain, wrote itself on the wall in front of her eyes, but she didn't believe it . . . she wouldn't believe it . . . didn't want it to be true.

It was midnight when the telephone rang. Kate was lying wakeful in bed. She took the steep little stairs at a run, snatched the receiver up. The caller was her father, John Christy. Oh, how like Pa, how typical of him to ring at this crazy hour!

'You don't sound pleased to hear me, Kate. Were you in bed and asleep?'

The line was bad, or his voice was faint. 'Pa dear, I'm thrilled to bits! Yes, I was in bed, but wide awake. Where are you speaking from? Brighton, I expect, I know you said you were playing there this week.' She spoke rapidly, disjointedly, thrusting her disappointment that the caller wasn't Ian out of her mind.

'Brighton was last week,' her father corrected. She heard him clearing his throat. 'We're in Newquay, Katie, we got here at eight tonight.'

'Goodness, but that's wonderful!' And now excitement swam in. She adored her father, the two of them were close. 'I seem to have got your dates muddled up,' she sounded apologetic, 'I thought it was next week you were coming to Cornwall.' She sat down on the stairs, holding the telephone on her knee.

'It was next week originally, but we managed to get away sooner. I don't start rehearsing for *Bland Justice* till the third week in September. The boys are on school holiday, and as Maxie sensibly said, the longer break will benefit us all.'

'Your voice sounds funny . . . you've got a cold.'

'It's a tired throat, that's all . . . nothing that rest and a change of scene and sea air won't cure. By the way, I saw Rose before we left Town, and she's as big as the side of a house. I shall be glad when she's had this baby of hers. She's not the strongest of mortals. Well, *you* know that, she's always been delicate.'

'She's tougher than you think, and she's having as much care as the Princess of Wales. Only around four weeks to go, and then you'll be a grandpa. How does that make you feel?'

'Not a great deal better,' he said without a vestige of a laugh. This was unlike him, very unlike. Kate felt a shoot of alarm.

'Pa, you *are* all right?'

'I've told you, yes. How's life on the grim, grim wards?'

'Not grim at all—a load of laughs.' And may Providence, she thought, forgive me for that very blatant lie. 'You haven't said when you're coming over. I'm dying to see you all.'

'We thought tomorrow, if that's all right.'

'Perfect, it's my weekend off.'

'We'll come mid-afternoon, then, around three o'clock. We'll have had our lunch before we start, so no need to fuss over food.'

Just a high tea around five, Kate thought, the kind of

meal little boys like. She asked her father if he would like to see Ellis Rand again. 'I did say I'd ask him round when you came to the cottage,' she told him.

'Of course, ask him . . . be delighted to see him.' Kate's letters to John Christy had mentioned Ellis Rand several times, and he wondered how friendly they were. He liked Rand—a clever young man—eccentric, a bit of a crank, but eccentrics and cranks were his bread and butter, so who was he to complain? She had also mentioned Ian Casson, which had made him ponder on a course of action he knew he ought to take. 'I must ring off, my darling,' he said, 'or Maxie will think I'm lost. Till tomorrow, then . . . love from us all.'

'Love to Maxine and the boys.'

''Night, Katie.' She heard his phone go down.

She replaced her own receiver, taking her time about it. Why should she have this feeling that all was not well with her father? Why should she feel that . . . why should she? He had said he was all right. He had sounded tired, but he often did at the end of a theatre run. He had had a long journey down here as well . . . that was all it was. She was getting as bad as Olly, with her silly premonitions. She went upstairs and got into bed, and tried to compose herself. But it was dawn, and the ancient rooster down at the Smugglers' Arms was bursting his throat in a raucous challenge to the streaks of light in the sky, before Kate finally managed to sleep.

CHAPTER NINE

'HE's had this hoarse voice for weeks,' Maxine said worriedly. It was the following day, and she and Kate were busy getting the tea. John Christy, Ellis, and the children were out in the garden, playing a game of baseball on the lawn. 'What do you think it is, Kate?' Maxine's silky dark hair tumbled forward, as she split and buttered rolls.

'Well, broadly speaking, laryngitis, but that's really just a symptom. It's the cause that matters. Has Pa had a cold, or any kind of infection?'

'No, he hasn't . . . nothing like that.'

'And he's managed to keep on working?'

'Yes, but last week at Brighton was hellish. I just don't know how he coped. And he won't see a doctor, he refuses to—says all he needs is a rest.'

'Actually, Maxine, he could be right,' Kate said thoughtfully. 'He could simply have a tired voice, but he ought to get it checked. All he may need is steam inhalations; it could be as simple as that. Hoarseness, in the ordinary way, is nothing to worry about, but it shouldn't persist, it shouldn't go on for weeks.'

'I wondered if you would talk to him,' Maxine bit her lip, 'you're a nurse, he'd be bound to listen to you. Perhaps he could see a doctor while we're down here . . . perhaps at your hospital?'

He could see Ian, flashed into Kate's mind. Who better than Ian? Pa had liked him, she well remembered their rapport in the past. 'Leave it to me,' she said to Maxine. 'I'll talk him round if I can, I'll do my best.'

130

'Oh, thank you, Kate . . . that's what I hoped you'd say! I knew I could rely on you.' Bowing her head on her arms, Maxine burst into tears. Kate stared at her aghast.

'Maxine, don't . . . please, Maxine, don't! Pa will be all right.' Kate stroked her stepmother's hair, while her heart thudded in fear. Why do we always think the worst? she asked herself helplessly. 'Together we'll see that he gets proper treatment, I promise you,' she said. 'Now let's finish getting this tea, shall we, and then we can join the others. The boys have grown, I can see a difference, even in only four months.' From the open doorway she watched Dick, who was seven, tearing round the lawn, legs going like pistons, hair dancing up and down. Roly, who was five, and who suited his name, being a little plump, was bottoms-up under the rhubarb leaves at the far end of the garden, frantically trying to extricate the ball. Ellis went to help him, her father stood waiting, legs apart, hands on hips—a craggy man with the light brown hair Kate had inherited. He could be stubborn, she knew that, and he had a way, at times, of deliberately turning his back on unpleasantness. Kate knew most of his weaknesses, and loved him not one whit less. Her mother had despised them, which was why, in the end, divorce had been the answer. Maxine adored him, just as he was; Kate rejoiced in their happy marriage. Please don't let him have anything serious, she begged.

They had a picnic tea in the garden, all eating up well, shadows and worries, for the moment, kept at bay. They were just at the finishing off stage, and the boys, under Ellis's guidance, were making darts out of serviettes, when a car drew up in the lane a few yards behind John Christy's Rolls. Its door swung wide, and even before she got to her feet Kate knew who it was . . . Ian, in flannels and open-necked shirt, backing out, then reaching into the car. Why had he come? Surprise vied with a state of warm confusion, which swept her from top to toe like a miniature storm. 'It's Ian,' she said, and began to walk over the lawn to meet him. By this time he was at the gate, fumbling with the catch. He was hampered by a long and awkward bouquet of gladioli and fern, which lay across him, cutting his shirt in two. Once inside the gate he stopped and stared in surprise at the crowd on the lawn. As well he might, Kate sympathised . . . what a motley, noisy crew! Her father had caught her up, and was already greeting Ian, stepping in front, shaking his hand, nearly capsizing the flowers.

'Good to see you again, Ian! Kate mentioned you in her letters. Great to see you . . . come and join us. It's a very long time since you last set eyes on Maxie and the boys.'

'I didn't know you were in Cornwall, sir.' Ian had little time to do more than smile a hello to Kate, before he was propelled towards the crowd around the tablecloth. He smiled at Maxine, taking her hand; he remembered her pale prettiness, the arresting beauty of her long-lashed violet eyes.

'We're here for a month,' she told him. 'John badly needs a rest.'

'We *both* need a rest,' John Christy corrected, turning to introduce Ellis, wondering why Kate put a quick hand on his arm.

'Ian and Ellis have already met, Pa,' she said, as Ian turned and placed the gladioli in her arms. She looked at them, they were beautiful—straight and tall and proud, pink and white, scarlet, and crimson-wine. 'They're absolutely gorgeous, Ian.'

'I grew them,' he said, 'cut them just now from my vegetable patch . . . sorry they're not gift-wrapped.'

'I prefer them like this.' She clasped them more

tightly, ridiculously glad that the flowers hadn't come from Helen's shop. 'Stay and have some tea, I can soon make some more.' Her father seconded this, but . . .

'No, I won't stop,' his tone was firm, 'I mustn't intrude on your party.' The boys had tired of their paper dart game and Ellis was giving Roly a pickaback ride down to the garden shed. 'As a matter of fact I'm on my way to Adela Norton's. I'm playing Lord Bountiful this afternoon, taking her some fruit. She's back at her own home now, here at Poldenack.'

He said goodbye to the others, and he must, Kate thought, have noticed Pa's voice, which, in a way, might make it easier for her to approach him when the time was opportune. She asked how Adela Norton was, as they walked to the gate. 'She seems all right . . . in great form,' he told her. 'Nell is staying with her for a short time, just for a week or two.'

'Good of her.'

'That's Nell all over.' Ian opened the gate and passed through. He stopped before he shut it, and seemed about to say more, then Dick came running up to Kate to show her a ladybird crawling in darkness between his two cupped hands. When she looked up Ian was by his car, stooping to get inside.

'Thank you again for the flowers,' she called, 'and remember me to Miss Norton.'

'Will do.' He lifted his hand and drove away.

Later that night, when everyone had gone, Kate arranged her stately flowers in a tall copper jug, which she set down in the hall. The spears of colour splayed out against the banisters. From there she would see them every time she went in and out of the cottage, or passed from the kitchen into the living-room. He had thought of her, he must have done, or he wouldn't have called in, even if he *were* on the way to someone else. He had thought of her when he cut the flowers. She acknowledged how much that pleased her . . . crumbs of comfort. Had she forgotten all those resolutions to stand away, not to become involved? And somehow . . . *somehow* . . . she had got to get Pa to see him. She had got to act as intermediary; she must approach her father first, when she went to Newquay to have dinner with him next week. But Fate was to take a hand in this, and its inescapable workings began on Monday when Ian came on to the ward.

He came when Kate was in the day room, talking to Mrs Romer, who was going home the following afternoon. She saw him go into her office, she excused herself and joined him; he was sitting on the edge of her desk, looking down at the floor. He rose when she entered, then sat down again, this time on a chair. 'Good weekend?' he asked pleasantly.

'Very good indeed.' No white coat, she noticed, which meant he wouldn't be staying . . . well, naturally not, with no patients in her ward.

'I was glad to meet your father again. I'm a great fan of his. I think I've seen every television play he's ever appeared in.' He watched Kate seating herself at the desk.

'You'll be able to see him again in November. He's playing the lead in the adaptation of Ellis's novel,' she told him smilingly.

'And that, I'm sure, will boost Rand's stock.' The tartness of his voice, and his switch of mood, made her feel out of step.

'The boosting works both ways,' she told him, 'the part is perfect for Pa. It could have been written *for* him. Actors are very lucky when they happen on something so good.'

'I'm sure you know more about those things than I do,

Kate—but to get down to mundane matters, I would like, if I may, to fill up one of your side-wards again, as from tomorrow at noon.'

'Oh, yes, of course.' She tried not to sound too eager or relieved. Ian was sending another patient, more patients would follow. His confidence in her as Ward Sister was unimpaired . . . everything on the hospital front was fine.

'I've brought her notes with me. I've been seeing her in New Outpatients at the Clinic.' The slim green folder of notes changed hands. 'She's suffering from hoarseness, and examination shows the presence of papilloma which, as you know, are harmless warty growths. She'll need a general anaesthetic, but this type of thing is usually easy to remove with forceps passed through a laryngoscope. The condition is a nuisance, not serious, but it needs to be tackled; if not breathlessness can occur.'

'How long is she likely to be with us?' asked Kate.

'She'll be out within a week. She's a Miss Tranter, a schoolmistress—teaches infants, I understand.'

'I'll get the first of the side-wards ready.' Kate riffled through the notes, then laid them down, her thoughts inevitably dwelling on her father, whose throat condition seemed so similar. She was tempted to mention him to Ian now, but something held her back. I must talk to Pa first, she thought; it wouldn't be right to go behind his back. But in the end she did just that, because Ian, who was watching her face, and noting her air of preoccupation, brought the subject up.

'I noticed that your father's voice was showing signs of strain. I expect he's had a long theatre run, has been over-using it.'

'He says it's tiredness, that he needs his holiday.'

'What does his doctor day?'

'He hasn't seen him.'

'Not? Good lord, that's very unwise of him!' He returned to the desk and sat down again. 'How long has he been like that?'

'About six weeks.'

He gave a whistle. 'He should see a doctor, Kate. It must be extremely tiring for him, apart from anything else.'

'Maxine has tried her best to persuade him, but she says he won't listen. She says he's stubborn, which is true, of course, that's one of my father's traits. But I also think,' her frown deepened, she looked straight into Ian's eyes, 'I think he's scared, I think he's frightened, I think . . . I'm sure he thinks he's got something serious, something sinister, which might mean extensive surgery and put an end to his acting career for good.'

'Yes,' said Ian. 'Yes, I see.' And that was all he said for several seconds, then: 'Can't *you* bring some sort of pressure to bear? He'll surely take notice of someone who knows what they're talking about. Tell him there's a dozen different things that can cause huskiness. There's an eight-to-one chance he's got nothing serious.'

'I'm going to do that,' she told him steadily, 'Maxine asked me to. I'm going to try my best to get him to see Dr Riskerton, as a temporary resident. He's my doctor at Poldenack.'

'He's Adela Norton's doctor. I met him at her house the other day . . . I've also had referrals from him in the past. It's possible that *if* Mr Christy needs a specialist's opinion he may, in the end, be sent to me.'

'But, Ian, it's you I want him to see. I thought of you at once, straight off, when Maxine asked me to help. If he needs surgery it's you I want . . . I want you to do it!'

'It's what *he* wants, my dear,' he corrected.

'Yes, I . . . yes, I know.'

'If he needs surgery, and consents to it, he may opt for a Harley Street man. Remember he has a very eminent surgeon in his father-in-law.'

'Hugh, yes, but all the same . . .'

'And we're jumping the gun, you know. All he may need is a rest and Friar's Balsam inhalations every night before he goes to bed.'

'I pray that's it,' sighed Kate.

'Pull all the stops out, and get him to see Riskerton,' said Ian briskly, heading for the door. He turned just before he reached it. 'Oh, I nearly forgot,' he said, 'a second patient will be coming to you on Thursday of this week—another sinusitis case; her notes will come to you later. After next week I'm on leave until the fourteenth of August. Annika Weiss will take over in my stead.'

'Oh!' Kate couldn't hide her dismay. Ian came and touched her shoulder, his fingers moving over the stuff of her dress.

'Listen, Kate, and listen hard—should your father be sent to me, I shan't let him down, whatever happens. I'm not going far away—just into Somerset to stay with my people, and only for a week and a day. I would come back, if necessary, so don't look so distressed.'

'Thank you . . . I'm grateful.' Now *her* voice was hoarse, and somehow that made her laugh.

'You do *your* bit,' he said, and went out of the door.

As it happened there was no need for Kate to do anything at all. At eight o'clock that evening, when she was washing her hair, the telephone rang and, cursing mildly, she wrapped her head in a towel and went downstairs to answer it. It was practically certain to be her father—and if it is, she thought, now is as good a time as any to start to work on him. 'Tradstow 3198, Kathryn Browning speaking.' She kept one hand on her head to secure the towel.

'Kate . . . it's Ian.'

'I . . . thought it was Father.' The towel unrolled itself as she sat down rather suddenly on the stairs.

'Your father has just this minute rung me, wants to see me about his throat. I have his permission to talk to you about it; he gave me your telephone number. I didn't mention that you and I had discussed him already.'

'I'm glad you didn't,' said Kate.

'I explained to him about seeing a GP first. He's going along to Riskerton's surgery first thing tomorrow morning. If he needs a specialist's opinion then he's going to opt for me.'

'Good!' Kate said quickly, then, more thoughtfully: 'He must be more worried than I realised—to seek professional help, so soon after coming on holiday.'

'I was surprised when he rang me, but glad as well. I was glad he felt I could help him. I suppose, in a way, I was touched and flattered, Kate.'

As he said this she wondered how she could ever have thought him arrogant. Because he's not . . . not at all; he's a modest man, yet reassuringly confident in a way that conveys itself to others, she thought. After he had said goodbye and rung off, she sat for some time on the stairs, drying her hair, and wondering if she ought to contact her father. She decided not to; if he wanted to get in touch, he would surely do so. Maxine was the one he must turn to. I must sit back and wait, not agitate him more by fluffing about. She was worried, though, deeply so, and if Rose knew Pa was ill, she would go berserk. We must all try to keep it from Rose, she thought.

John Christy rang Kate at four-thirty next day; he needed her support. She was just on the point of going off duty; he sounded even more hoarse. 'I'm in Tradstow, Katie. I'm seeing Ian this evening at his rooms. Riskerton has referred me to him, contacted him by phone, fixed it all up, so the dreaded die is cast.'

'It's sensible to be tackling it, Pa.' She was holding the phone with one hand, pulling her cap off with the other; she had a sensation of dread. He had been referred . . . so there *was* something, something other than strain. 'You couldn't have a better man than Ian.'

'How about coming with me, along to his rooms?' suggested her father. 'Maxie had to go back to Newquay, on account of the boys. Being the shocking coward I am . . .'

'Darling, of course I'll come with you, of course I'll come! What time are you due?'

'Half-five.' He cleared his throat.

'Let's have tea first. Meet me at Grants, it's just round the corner from Ian. There's a coffee house called Flavia's next door. I'll be there in fifteen minutes. We can park the cars too, there's a decent space at the back.'

'Good idea.' John Christy rang off, and over tea at Flavia's he confided some of his worst fears to his younger daughter, Kate. 'If I'm going to be ill, if I'm going to snuff it . . .' a strong sense of the dramatic was inherent in his make-up, he exploited it even then, 'I would rather it were down here in Cornwall. This is where I belong, my roots are here. I was born and brought up in the cottage you're living in now.'

'Yes, Pa, I know you were, and I think I know what you mean.'

'You always do,' he said simply; Kate's eyes strayed to the clock.

'We ought to be moving, ten minutes to go.' Shortly after that they were mounting the flight of steps to Ian's front door.

Miss Latham, who was fiftyish, grey-haired and brisk, opened the door to their ring. 'Mr Casson is on the phone at the moment, he won't be long,' she said. She showed them into the waiting-room, leading off from the office, where Kate had worked that June evening, seven weeks ago, and had reached a time of crisis in her life.

She and her father sat in club chairs, both feeling as strung up as each other. He looks so ill . . . Kate glanced at him. He was drawn, and gaunt, and resigned. His air of resignation was the most frightening thing of all. Why did she have to keep thinking of Danny? Pa wasn't going to die. Averting her eyes, she concentrated on a water-colour painting of Bedruthan Sands which hung on the opposite wall.

When the door opened and Ian stepped in, it was Kate who shot to her feet, not John Christy, who eased himself out of his chair like a tired old man. If Ian was surprised to see Kate there, he gave no sign of it. He greeted them both, and apologised for keeping his patient waiting. He took him into the consulting-room and Miss Latham joined them there; Kate heard her go, doors were closed, and not a sound filtered through them. She went to the table and picked up a magazine. It was one of the glossies, slippery and awkward; her nervous fingers dropped it. She picked it up and replaced it on its pile. Crossing to the window, she stared out at the hospital opposite—at the Royal ENT Clinic, built in Dickens' time. The two wings had been added in the late nineteen-thirties. One was still in its scaffolding shell, after the lorry crash; the other, Kate knew, was the private wing, more often called Morland House. If her father had to undergo surgery, would he go into that wing? He would probably wish to, he was well-known . . . famous, and the very last thing he would want would be any undue publicity, so difficult to avoid in one of the many-bedded NHS wards.

Hearing a faint sound behind her, she turned to see Miss Latham, still brisk, still smiling, trim as a bird, standing in the doorway, holding a clipboard and pushing her glasses up. 'Mr Casson and Mr Christy would like you to join them now. She held the door wide, and Kate crossed the hall to the big consulting-room. The distance felt miles, and her father and Ian, who both stood up when she entered, looked far away, like puppets on a stage. Her father was smiling, he held out his hands. 'It's all right, my darling,' they all sat down, 'there's no carving-up to be done!'

'Not?' She looked at Ian, registering the fact that his face was wearing the amiable ungive-away look she had seen so many times on Penhallow Ward.

'I've told him to let you in on everything that's amiss with me,' John Christy said. Ian was behind his desk, but he came round to the front and sat with them, talking, mainly, to Kate.

'Your father has a vocal nodule, Kate, which has manifested itself as a small white point on the edge of his vocal cords. As I'm sure you know, this condition can occur from overworking the voice. With complete rest it will disappear, go away on its own. Without rest—if your father continues to strain, as he is now, to make himself heard, the node will enlarge and have to be removed. Now, as he's anxious to avoid surgery, I've suggested, and he agrees, that he goes into Morland House for a stay of two to three weeks. He needs *total* rest, no talking at all—he must communicate by signs, and by pad and pencil; nothing less stringent is going to do the trick. If he continues his holiday at the hotel, he'll naturally try to talk, it would be inevitable, he could hardly be off it, and quite apart from his voice, Mr Christy is stressed from overwork; he needs partial bed rest and quiet.'

'Otherwise I'm in for a breakdown,' John Christy croaked.

'It's possible,' Ian agreed.

'It's hard on my wife . . . holidaying on her own.'

'She'll have the boys,' Kate put in gently, 'and this I can truly tell you—Maxie will be over the moon that there's nothing radically wrong. She's been out of her mind, terribly worried.'

'Yes, I know she has. All right then, Ian, go ahead, make your diabolical plans. Whatever you say, I'll go along with, I'll put myself in your hands.'

'Good! We'll go across the road and make the arrangements now; there's nothing like the present.' Ian's eyes met Kate's. Without being told she knew that he was thinking the same as she was . . . get everything sewn and buttoned up before he changes his mind . . . with which course of action she firmly agreed.

John Christy went into Morland House on Wednesday at noon. Maxine drove him in from Newquay, and afterwards she and Kate lunched together near the City Hospital. As Kate had surmised, Maxine was thankful that her husband had agreed to rest. 'I can see him each evening,' she said. 'I'll make arrangements for the boys to be minded from teatime onwards. The hotel provides those facilities, which is partly why we chose it. Oh, and by the way, Kate, if you should be approached by any reporters, refer them to me. John has told me exactly what to say.'

'Is that likely to happen?' Kate's eyes opened wide.

'I don't know, but it's possible. Within hours of our arrival at the Talland Head Hotel we had a girl reporter approach us. I suppose that's the price of fame, but the last thing John wants is a story going round that he's been taken ill. I shall have to let his agent know, but even that I'll play down. You *do* understand?'

'Yes, of course I do. I'll be very careful, Maxine. If anything leaks it won't be my fault—I'll be discretion itself. Anyway, very few people down here know I'm John Christy's daughter. As for Ian, he would just raise his brows and say "no comment". I don't honestly think the Press will get hold of it.'

But they did, for on Friday the *Tradstow Times* carried, on its third page, a small paragraph headed ACTOR JOHN CHRISTY COLLAPSES ON HOLIDAY. Underneath appeared in smaller type: The well-known theatre and television actor, John Robert Christy, was admitted to the private wing of the Royal Hospital, Tradstow, on Wednesday of this week, after loss of voice and a breakdown in his health. He is likely to be in hospital several weeks.'

Ellis drew Kate's attention to it. He brought the paper round as soon as he heard her drive in on Friday night. She had not seen him since Sunday, when they had joined forces with Eve and her current boy-friend, and gone swimming off Tolcarne beach. 'Is it true?' he asked, his frown deep. Kate did not answer at once; she was too intent on reading the paragraph.

'In essence it's true . . . yes, Ellis, but I'm also perfectly sure this isn't the statement Maxine would have given out.'

'How ill is he, exactly?' Ellis sounded belligerent.

'Not as ill as this implies, but you saw him on Saturday, you must have noticed that he didn't look well; you must have noticed his voice.'

'I assumed he was getting over a cold.'

'Pa's been overworking,' Kate told him. 'Had he not consented to treatment, he might have become very ill. As it is he's got to rest up for the next two or three weeks.'

'Is he going to be fit to start rehearsals for *Bland Justice* in September?'

'I'm sure he will.' She looked at Ellis's frowning,

disgruntled face. He was plainly more annoyed than sorry that her father was ill. Yet on Saturday he had appeared delighted to meet him and Maxine again. He had got on well with the children too. Had that just been an act? But surely now, at the very least, he could say what bad luck it was, go through the ordinary motions of being polite. She watched him take the offending paper and his boorish mood back to his cottage. She tried to find excuses for him; perhaps he had had a bad day, and was fed-up and tired, exactly like herself.

'On the whole,' said Ian next day, when he came on to the ward, 'your father reacted fairly calmly to the news item about him. I expected a hoarse explosion, whereas all I got in the end were two very telling swear-words written on his pad, in capital letters, and heavily under-lined.'

'Oh, poor Pa! But at least I'm glad he didn't hit the roof.'

'It was a great pity it had to happen . . . the news item, I mean. But it's very, very difficult to keep anything like that quiet. There's usually someone who'll talk to the press, given a little encouragement.'

'I understand that, and so will he. How's he getting on?'

'Doing as he's told, at present, using pad and pencil, and sign language, as though he were born to it. The nodule can still be seen at the junction with the middle third cord—the exact place where the cords need to hit together to produce sound. It should go in a week, perhaps less than that, but aside from the throat aspect, Kate, your father's very low in health, entirely due to fatigue. Steve Saint, our consultant physician, is looking after that side. He and Annika will take good care of him while I'm in Somerset. I go tomorrow, Sunday . . . I'll see him before I set off.'

'Thank you for all you're doing for him,' said Kate.

'It happens to be my job,' he said dismissively, one eye on the clock.

'I'm sure you need your holiday,' she gave him Miss Tranter's notes, 'but eight days isn't very long, is it?'

'Better than nothing at all. I'm due for more leave later on when the Clinic rebuilding programme has been completed, and then, of course, I'll be back there all the time.'

'I expect you'll be glad.'

'To be back there . . . yes, in some ways I will, but I'll miss seeing you.'

'And I you,' Kate said quickly, but the little exchange of words was no more than that . . . Ian wasn't even looking her way at the time; he was frowning down at Miss Tranter's treatment sheet.

She wondered, later, as she saw his car easing out of the gates, if Helen would be going with him to Somerset to visit his parents. She most likely would, if Adela Norton was well enough to be left. Leaving her own car on the park, she made her way round to the Creamery. There she met Maxine, and afterwards they went to visit John Christy—'the Dumb-bell', as he described himself on his pad.

CHAPTER TEN

THE Sunday service had just begun in the day room when Nurse Heston came to tell Kate that she was wanted urgently on the phone. 'It's a personal call, Sister—a Mrs Clevington.' Kate hurried back to the office. What on earth was Rose thinking about, ringing her at the hospital? It was always understood that she confined her calls to home. She snatched up the phone. 'Rose? Kate here,' she said.

Rose wasted no time on preliminaries. She was very, very distressed. 'I've just seen the paper . . . Daddy's ill; Why ever didn't you tell me? I want to know exactly what's wrong. What do they mean by breakdown? Is he seriously ill . . . you've got to tell me! I saw it in the *Express*!'

For goodness' sake, why didn't I realise that one of the Sunday papers might get hold of that news item about Pa? Kate fumed. Making herself calm down, she hurried to reassure Rose, telling her step by step exactly what was wrong with their father, and why he would be in hospital for a while.

'You're not being *professional*, hiding the truth?' Rose's voice was shrill.

'No, and Rose, I'm sorry I didn't . . .'

'Did Ian find the growth?'

'It's not a growth, I told you that.'

'Well, I don't like the sound of it. I shall get Hugh to ring Ian direct. I think you're fobbing me off. If it was something and nothing, why didn't you tell me, right from the very beginning? He's my father as well as yours

146

. . . you don't have sole rights!' Rose rang off. She had sounded hysterical.

'But she was right, of course, I should have told her. I made a wrong decision,' Kate said to Ian when he put his head round her door. The Professor had phoned him just as he was about to leave for Somerset. They had talked for some minutes, then Rose had had her say. She had been so concerned about her father that any awkward-ness which might have manifested itself, bearing in mind past happenings, was non-existent, just simply wasn't there. What Ian had felt was a mixture of exasperation and affection. Rose had felt worried, puzzled, and cross in just about equal proportions. Why on earth hadn't her father consulted Hugh in London, and been admitted to the Walbrook Hospital? If the self-same query reared itself in Hugh Clevington's mind, he gave no indication of it as he talked and listened to Ian, his one-time Registrar and friend.

'With your father's permission I gave the Prof the salient medical facts, and he in his turn will calm Rose down, I very much hope,' said Ian, as he sat in front of Kate's desk. His telephone conversation with Hugh had brought memories flooding back, the good ousting the bad in their hundreds, he had felt a sense of release . . . yes, that was it, a sense of release, as though a very long worry-cord had been cut in two and flung away for good.

'Praise my Soul, the King of Heaven,' filtered through from the day room. The service would be over in a few moments, the Chaplain would be coming out, looking for a cup of coffee with the Sister on Penhallow Ward, before going on to St Michael's Church. Aware of this, Kate could not help an involuntary glance behind her, through her viewing window, into the ward.

'You want to get on, don't you?' Ian's voice sounded amused.

'I'm glad you came.'

'But you'd like me to go?' He was feigning fear of her, hunching his shoulders and creeping to the door. He was plainly in a lighthearted mood, a holiday mood, she supposed. And who could blame him? He must be glad to leave patients and problems behind him, and drive away from trouble for the brief space of eight days.

Steps sounded outside the door, followed by a tap, and the faint sliding of cups on saucers, as Jean Betts, the voluntary helper, balanced her tray, waiting for Sister's permission to go in. As she came in, Ian went out, smiling goodbye to Kate over the top of Mrs Betts' beehive head.

The following day, and the one after that, were Kate's days off. On Monday she went to the supermarket in Poldenack's main street; the contents of her fridge were getting low. It was a beastly day for the second week in August; a thick sea mist was spreading over the little town, distorting traffic sounds and making the crossing of even a very narrow road hazardous. And I ought to have had more sense, she thought, than to bother with the car, but walking up the steep hill to her cottage, laden with a week's groceries, was something she always tried to avoid.

In the supermarket, at the frozen foods section, she spotted Miss Adela Norton in corduroy trousers and a fisherman's jersey, bending over the cabinets, trying to reach something at the back. She jumped, startled, when Kate touched her elbow, and as she straightened and turned, Kate was equally startled to see how much older she looked; her face was tramlined and she gave the appearance of not having slept all night. Had Helen gone to Somerset with Ian? Was the old lady all on her own? And if she was, she shouldn't be; she was plainly far from well. She looked at Kate in a bemused fashion, then: 'Sister Browning!' she exclaimed. She half-smiled and touched her arm, and Kate got the firm impression that she was glad to see her, which was certainly something new.

'Can I help you with your shopping, Miss Norton?' She took her wire basket and put it on top of her own laden trolley. 'If this is your last shop, I would be pleased to drive you home. It's a horrible damp day to be out.'

'All right, yes,' was her grudging reply, which was rather more in keeping with her usual offhand manner than her distrait greeting had been. Yet even now she would like to refuse me, Kate thought, as she steered Miss Norton, and the trolley, towards the nearest till.

A few minutes later, with their shopping stacked on the back seat of the Fiat, they crawled through the mist towards Station Road, which was where Miss Norton lived. It was a short journey, but an eerie one, with visibility down to a matter of yards, making talking impossible. The foghorn on the lighthouse was wailing away like a banshee, the sea was invisible, merging with the sky.

Miss Norton's house was semi-detached, snow-cemmed, tall and thin. She asked Kate in, and it was there, in her kitchen, warm from an Aga range, that she told her about the terrible news Helen had received on Sunday, soon after they were up. 'Her parents were in a car crash on Saturday night, Sister Browning . . . in America, just outside Boston, they were coming home from a party. We heard about it by telephone, a transatlantic call from one of their friends. He said they were both very badly injured; they were in hospital and they weren't expected to live. Helen was dreadfully shocked, poor girl; she rang Mr Casson's house. He wasn't there, but she managed to catch him at one of the hospitals. He came straight here, and was on the telephone for what seemed to be hours and hours, trying to get her a flight; she wanted to go at once. In the end he got a double cancellation for early this morning and they travelled all night to Gatwick; they should be airborne now.'

'I'm so sorry! What a dreadful shock for Helen, and for you as well. I remember you saying . . .'

'Helen's mother, Marie, is very dear to me. I was young when I brought her up, she was like my own baby, like my own child.' Miss Norton's eyes glimmered with difficult tears. 'She's been very good to me, always has me to stay when they're over here in England . . . always at Christmas and Easter . . . that was the last time I saw her. If I had a passport I'd go to her.' Miss Norton turned her back and began to move a kettle and saucepan over the top of the stove. 'You may as well have a drink while you're here.' Her voice sounded cracked and old. 'I usually have milk, but you can have tea.'

'Thank you.' Kate got up to help her.

'I can manage, thanks.' Miss Norton was ever-independent. What she needed was reassurance, and Kate strove to give her that.

'Helen may find,' she said quietly, 'that her parents' injuries are not nearly so bad as at first feared. And so much can be done by clever doctors and surgeons, these days, so try not to worry too much. Remember you've been very ill yourself.'

'I'm old, it doesn't matter.'

'It matters a very great deal!'

The old lady sniffed . . . in disdain this time, but Kate fancied her face looked less ravaged as they sat down with their drinks.

'Will you be all right on your own?' she asked her, just before she left.

'Perfectly. Why shouldn't I be? I've got the telephone. Helen had it put in only last week, not that it's brought me much joy . . . only terrible news, so far.' She cast a baleful glance at the brand-new dark green instrument through in the hall. Kate gave her her own telephone number.

'Ring me, if you need help,' she said.

'Thank you, Sister . . . kind of you.'

'You could try calling me Kate!' But Miss Norton didn't appear to have heard her, she was already closing her door and retreating inside out of the seeping mist.

The local train from Tradstow—a diesel—hawed its way into the station, as Kate drove away from the tall, thin house. She felt very sorry for Adela Norton, even more sorry for Helen. She brought to mind a conversation she and Helen had had in the ward a few weeks ago, when Miss Norton was a patient. Helen had asked about Danny, and had followed Kate's reply with the comment that she had never lost anyone close. I just hope she's not going to do so now, Kate thought as Bob Nansock's taxi passed her, filmed in mist, and pipping its horn. Ian had gone to America with Helen, he was helping her all he could; he had gone to America and dispensed with his Somerset holiday, just like that. He must think a very great deal of her—the whole world, in fact. But how terrible to feel jealous of Helen at an awful time like this! I'm small-minded, petty and jealous . . . all the things I hate the most. He loves Helen, just bear that in mind, he loves Helen Reever. Sometimes trouble brings people closer. She thought of them in the plane, sitting together, sharing the worry, the torment of uncertainty. Helen had turned to Ian in her pain.

She spent the rest of the day doing chores, cleaning the little cottage with an avid, violent thoroughness; she couldn't bear to be still. She cleaned the windows inside and out, she even washed two blankets, shampooed a carpet, and painted a cupboard door. In the early evening, with the mist long gone, she went down to the beach and swam. She relaxed at last, moving idly through the gently swelling water, warm as milk, softly hushing, a caress on tired limbs. There had to be other things in life besides loving a man. For the brief space of an hour she was content.

It was quiet back at the cottage, for Ellis was away, seeing his agent and publisher in London. He had gone off late last night. He was never very much in evidence, yet Kate missed that undefinable, companionable feeling of having someone next door. She missed the rattle of his typewriter too, and when she woke in the night she could not, for the moment, think why it was that everything seemed so quiet. Had she known it, that quietude was to be of short duration. A little after five-thirty a shaking, thunderous knocking sounded on her front door, followed by a shout. Heart in mouth, she leapt out of bed and over to the window. There on the path was Bob Nansock, a case in either hand, and beside him was . . . beside him was . . . *Rose and her mother!* Rose and Mummy . . . but why, and what . . . Kate was down the stairs in seconds, unbolting the door, clicking back the lock, taking off the chain.

'Mummy! Rose! Whatever . . .' They hugged and laughed and exclaimed. Grinning to himself, Bob Nansock climbed back into his taxi. They had been lucky to catch him just like that. He had gone along to the station to pick up a geyser who hadn't turned up. He was pleased with the tip he'd got—Audrey Christy had been in a generous mood.

'I had to come and see Daddy, Kate—I couldn't just leave it. I had to come and see for myself exactly how he is.' They were all three in the sitting-room, Rose was on the settee, feet up; she and her mother had been in the train all night. 'We couldn't get a sleeper at such short notice . . .just look how my legs have swelled!'

'I'm looking,' Kate said grimly. 'Rose, you're very near your time.'

'There was no stopping her coming,' Audrey Christy broke in. 'Hugh couldn't get away, he's got a heavy list all this week. I had to drop everything, or she'd have come down on her own.'

'I could have managed. I'm four whole weeks away from my EDD—which in case you don't know the term, is my expected delivery date,' Rose patted her front and smoothed it into a round.

'I *do* know . . . . I've done midwifery!' Kate couldn't help laughing at her.

'Just as well . . . might come in useful!' And Rose, Kate thought, was far more lively than her mother, who looked haggard and fatigued.

'I'm only here for the night,' she said, 'I'll have to go back tomorrow. Rose wants to stay till today week, when Hugh can get down to fetch her. Can you stretch to that kind of hospitality, with all your other commitments?'

'Oh, Mummy! What a question!'

'Rose will be safe with you . . . safely protected. I told Hugh that.' As both women yawned, Kate suggested baths and bed.

'The immersion's been on all night. I'll bring your breakfasts upstairs. You'll have to use my bed, Rose, and Mummy can have the spare room. I must have had a premonition that you two would be coming. I had a terrific clean and spruce-up yesterday.'

'Are you on holiday?' Rose asked sleepily, rolling up off the sofa.

'No, I'm on duty tomorrow.'

'I want to see Daddy tonight.'

'First things first.' Kate took charge, she saw them

both up to their rooms, then came back and started preparing trays. Rose wanted a proper fry-up, she said, which meant bacon and egg and tomato, and a sausage perhaps; she got them all out of the fridge.

Her mother, in nightgown and negligee, joined her in the kitchen. 'I'll have mine down here with you, Kate, and nothing cooked for me, just toast and coffee, and some juice if you've got it. I'm sorry about this invasion, I'm sorry I couldn't give you warning, but Rose said you'd fuss, and try to stop us because of the baby.'

'Well, she *is* a bit near,' Kate demurred.

'She's also very determined. She meant it, you know, when she said she would have come on her own. Hugh and I had such a job with her. I had to down tools and come. She adores her father.'

'Yes, I know.' Kate broke an egg in the pan.

'How is he, really?' asked Audrey.

'Exactly as Ian told Rose and Hugh over the phone. It's a matter of absolute quiet and rest, then he'll be just fine.'

'Interesting for you to meet Ian again. You two always got on.'

'Yes, I suppose we did, in a way.'

Audrey Christy's look was shrewd. 'I thank God he and Rose didn't marry. He was totally wrong for her. He would never have had patience with all her capriciousness. Rose, bless her heart, can be awfully trying; Hugh delights in her vagaries. They're a happy couple, they mix and match. I'm very nearly envious.' She was watching Kate closely as she set up Rose's tray.

'I'll get this to her, while it's hot.'

'There's enough for a baby rhino!' Mrs Christy laughed, sipping her grapefruit juice.

By nine o'clock both Rose and her mother, curtains drawn over their windows, were sleeping off the effects of their night in the train. Kate moved quietly about the cottage, making lists and plans, and telephoning Maxine, keeping her voice down low. Audrey Christy wanted to see her ex-husband, which was fair enough, Kate supposed, but even so, she ought to tell Maxine, just in case of awkward moments. Maxine and her mother *had* met, but not for several years, not since Roly had been a babe in arms. Also her father ought to be warned that two wives would be coming . . . well, more less; Kate explained it all on the phone. Maxine's reaction was spontaneous; she laughed, blowing away Kate's anxiety. 'Oh, Kate, really! We're civilised people . . . of *course* I don't mind,' she said. 'I'll bring the boys, it won't hurt them to be late to bed for once. John's allowed to speak in a whisper, as from last night. The node thing's practically disappeared, so Mrs Weiss told me when I rang just now, but she's playing safe till Ian Casson gets back. I'll ring John now, and tell him about the expected influx. I'm not really all that surprised, you know, that Rose has come down here, and John will be pleased to see her, you can be assured of that.'

'That's true, and Maxine, how marvellous that he's getting right at last.' After a little more conversation, and catching Maxine's mood, Kate rang off and began to plan menus again.

'There's nothing like having six visitors when I'm only allowed two,' John Christy chuckled early that evening, when they all filed in behind Sister Bonham, who plainly disapproved. Dick and Roly rushed at their father, whom they had not seen for a week, then climbed into an armchair, giggling behind their hands. John Christy was up, at a table by the window, wearing a heavy silk dressing-gown of dark crimson, with velvet facings and cuffs. He had an air of the theatre about him, so maybe he felt, thought Kate, that a little acting was necessary to get him through the evening. Rose moved towards him and was folded in his arms. 'Well, who's a foolish girl, then?' he whispered, kissing her face and hair. Maxine sat at the table with him, and Audrey and he exchanged greetings; they kissed too; Kate was watching points. Roly wanted to sit on his knee, but Maxine held him off. 'Daddy doesn't want a big boy like you bouncing all over him! Come over here and look out of the window, look at that lovely fountain, and the little mermaid sitting on a stone.'

Kate had never admired Maxine more than she did at that moment. With enormous tact and diplomacy she had left the stage to Rose and her mother, to talk to Pa, in the few moments they had. I wonder if I would be as generous and as unjealous as that, in similar circumstances, she wondered, as they drove back to the cottage. Maxine knows she has Pa's love, she's secure in that knowledge. Her mother was rather quiet, she thought; the only comment she made was on how like John the little boys were.

As Kate was on lates duty next day, she was able to see her off on the early morning express train from Tradstow to Paddington. They left Rose in bed; it had been agreed she would stay there till noon each day, then visit her father during the afternoons. She would go by taxi, and Kate would pick her up from Morland House at five o'clock when she left the hospital.

'Thank you, darling, for bearing with Rose. You're always so reliable.' Audrey Christy paid Kate this rare compliment, as they sat in the train, whiling away the five minutes before it would start. 'Hugh will ring her every evening, and he'll come down on Tuesday . . . or rather, Monday, getting the same night train that Rose and I did.'

'I know, Mummy—you've told me all this at least a

dozen times. I love having Rose, so no need to worry. It's unlike you to be jumpy. There's nothing *else* worrying you, is there?' Once again she was struck by something undefinably different about her mother's manner. She felt anxious. She moved over to her side.

'Actually there is,' Mrs Christy half-smiled. 'I'm trying to make a decision—rather an important one, as it happens. Edward Jules wants us to marry. He wants to cement our partnership, make it real, he says. There's a strong bond between us, Kate. We think alike on things. We've been business partners now for nearly fifteen years, as you know. Since his wife died he's been lonely, and I know that feeling too. I'm seriously thinking of saying "yes" despite the considerable age gap—Edward is twenty years older than me.'

He's an old man, flashed into Kate's mind, then as quickly out again. What a mean thought! Seventy was nothing, especially in a man. She knew Mr Jules, she had met him often . . . a grey-haired, distinguished man, with impeccable manners, and beautiful suits. He had two grown-up sons, and grandchildren too . . . three or four. 'Mummy, if you love him . . .'

'I'm fond of him, we get along, we're very *compatible*, Kate.' Mrs Christy paused for a moment, then quickly carried on: 'People marry for all sorts of reasons, every marriage is different. I was glad to see your father yesterday, partly because of this. It seemed important to meet him again—not to help me make up my mind, but to make sure I felt entirely free. It's difficult to explain, even for a middle-aged woman with a legal mind!'

'Yes, I can see.' Kate was getting her breath back.

'Rose doesn't know as yet. I've talked about it to no one but Edward . . . well, naturally, I've talked to him . . . so keep my secret till I know what I'm going to do.' They kissed quickly and bumpily, then Kate tumbled out, as the train began to make juddery noises, getting ready to go. She stood on the platform as it passed from the station, till all that remained of it was its ochre end dwindling tunnelwards.

The news that her mother had just let slip—on impulse, Kate felt sure—occupied her mind, as she drove back to Poldenack. If she marries Edward Jules what a complicated family we'll be with all the step and half relationships! she thought. She was sure her father would approve, though, not without a pang. Rose might be difficult at first, but she'd come round in the end. Edward Jules and Hugh would get on. There was no doubt about it, Kate was rapidly warming to the idea. She wished she could talk to Rose about it—but my lips are sealed, she thought, using one of her father's turns of phrase.

But when she got home, and picked up the morning newspaper from the mat, even the thought of her mother's possible marriage sailed out of her head. The bottom of the front page bore the headline: 'PELAPAS Chairman Dies'. Underneath she read: 'Mr Garfield Reever, Chairman and Managing Director of Pelapas Chemicals Limited, died in Boston, Massachusetts, yesterday, following injuries sustained in a car accident last Saturday. His wife, Geraldine Marie Reever, remains critically ill. Members of the family and friends are by her side.

Kate took the paper into the kitchen while she prepared Rose's breakfast tray. She would have to go round and see Miss Norton before she went on duty. What sad news . . . how awful for them all!

CHAPTER ELEVEN

OLLY was full of the tragedy when Kate saw him on Thursday. He had been on days off, during which time he had seen his friends the Carringtons. 'Harold Carrington and his son have flown out,' he told Kate over lunch. 'They were all away touring in France when the accident happened, you know, and they didn't get back until Monday night. Harold and Mrs Reever are first cousins. I gather she's very ill.'

'Poor woman, and the news of her husband's death isn't likely to help.' Kate picked at her fish, which seemed to be full of bones.

'He'll be a great loss to industry,' said Olly, professing an understanding of such matters as big business, which Kate felt fairly sure he didn't possess. 'I understand Mr Casson went to Boston with Helen Reever,' he added, looking over at Kate.

'Yes, so Miss Norton told me.'

'She'll be upset, I'll be bound.'

'Terribly. I feel sorry for her. I went round to see her, but there's not much I can do except sympathise. I've got my sister with me this week, so I'm just a little bit tied. I don't like leaving her alone in the evenings, she's eight and a half months pregnant. She came to see Father, there was no way of stopping her.'

'Perhaps they're close,' suggested O.B.

'They are,' said Kate, as they left the canteen together and made their way downstairs to the wards.

Hugh telephoned Rose every single evening promptly at eight o'clock. They would talk for ages, after which

Rose would return to the sitting-room starry-eyed, and full of London news. 'Only three more days, and he'll be here to fetch me,' she said on Friday evening. 'It's so awful being apart, Katie, especially at such a time.' She eased herself crabwise on to a chair.

'I expect it is,' Kate agreed.

'I wish I could have met Ellis Rand while I was here,' said Rose. 'Daddy was telling me you two had got friendly.'

'Yes,' Kate said, 'we have.' She was trying to write to their mother; she looked at Rose, pen in hand.

'Anything in it?' asked Rose.

'Nothing but friendship.'

'Pity,' she said. 'It's a high time you fell in love again. You can't *still* be mourning Danny; he's been dead for eighteen months. If the boot were on the other foot, *he* would have married again.'

'Don't talk about what you don't understand,' Kate said crossly, feeling irked. Undeterred, Rose rattled on; she seldom saw danger-spots; at times she could be extremely insensitive.

'And Ian has to be away too,' she said, 'just as I'm down this way. Is he in love with this Reever girl he's gone to America with?'

'I've no idea,' Kate said shortly, 'and you can't keep tabs on him, Rose. You can't throw him over, and expect him to pine away for evermore. Ian's emotions run deep, I'm sure, but he's very practical too. What he knows he can't have, he can put behind him, and start all over again.'

Rose stared at her, and the baby nightgown she was busily sewing dropped from her hands, her blue eyes opened wide. 'Actually, Kate, you've got it all wrong,' she said quietly. 'Ian and I started coming apart as soon as we got engaged. I know that sounds extraordinary, but that was the way it was. Differences began to show up then, that we simply couldn't . . . settle. I know you think I treated him badly, but one divorce in the family is quite enough. I know I did the right thing.'

'You did the right thing in the wrong way!'

'Oh *well*, you'd take his side. You're as bossy in your way as he is in his.' Rose smiled at her sister. She seemed remarkably tranquil about it all.

Monday—her last full day in Cornwall, and Ian's last day of absence—dawned fine and bright, and very still, with an ultra clearness of light, which very often presaged storm and gale. The summer gales in this part of the world could be as fierce as the winter ones; they could turn the sea to surf-flecked mountains, they could roar across the peninsula, carrying salty spray for miles inland. But it was calm enough when Kate set off for the hospital that morning, promising to collect Rose from Morland House at five. Hugh was getting the night train from London, and would arrive at the cottage at dawn on Tuesday, just as Rose and her mother had done. He would then have the journey all the way back, with Rose, of course, at midday. After which I should think the poor man will be suffering from train-lag, Kate thought, turning in at the hospital gates.

The big ward was full again, the patients all William Jarman's. One of the side-wards was empty, as Miss Tranter had been discharged. Mrs Colton, the sinusitis patient, on whom Annika Weiss had operated, would most likely be going home next day, after Ian had seen her. 'The tube will have to stay in her nostrils for some weeks yet,' Annika explained to Kate, 'but it shouldn't bother her much. It's vital it should stay in place till fibrosis has ended. She knows this and accepts it; she says she's only thankful to be free of that awful pressuring pain. Most likely Ian will want to admit another patient this week. He's back tomorrow, as you know. 'She looked over her shoulder at Kate. 'Have you heard from him?'

'No.' Kate shook her head.

'I don't think anyone has. He's most likely been busy, and had no time for writing dirty postcards. I'm sure he'll discharge your father either tomorrow or Wednesday. Those two weeks in Morland House have done wonders for Mr Christy. Quite apart from his voice, all the other little health flaws that could have become big ones have been corrected with treatment. Dr Saint has played his part there. It was a case of a stitch in time, really.'

'You've been marvellous, Mrs Weiss,' Kate told her.

'I like your father. It was a privilege to look after him,' she said. 'When is your sister's baby due?' Annika Weiss had seen Rose on one or two occasions at Morland House.

'In three weeks' time.'

'You *hope*!' said Annika, teasing Kate a little. 'With a primigravid patient it could be early, or late.'

'I certainly hope the latter,' laughed Kate, opening her office door. 'My brother-in-law, who's arriving tomorrow, would feel immensely cheated if she beat him to it—he wants to be present, every inch of the way.'

'He's Professor Clevington, isn't he—Ian's old chief? Ian attributes much of his success to the Professor's influence.'

'He's a success in his own right now.'

'I agree with that, plus-plus,' said Annika, going off to Olly's ward.

All throughout the week Kate had been trying to tell herself how much better it was without Ian, how much more calm she felt. Life had almost reverted to the way it had been when she first came to Cornwall, with every-thing running smoothly, without a single ripple to disturb the careful routine of her day. She knew, though, what a mammoth slice of self-deception this was. She had missed him, missed preparing for him, listening for his step, missed the rush of excitement and thrill when he came in suddenly. It had seemed a very long week indeed, even with Rose at the cottage. It had had its pleasant moments, with her father getting well, and having Eve Sawyer round to supper—she and Rose had got on well, but the days had lacked savour, they were simply days, just hours, and minutes and seconds of plodding on, getting done, getting through without him. But at least, she thought, this time has prepared me for when he will no longer come. It's prepared me for when the rebuilding work at the Clinic is over and done. This week has been a kind of preparation, or rehearsal, for that. I shall never see him afterwards, except by pure chance . . . just to nod and smile at, when I meet him in the town. The telephone ringing stopped her musings, and she pulled herself together, and answered a prescription query from Pharmacy.

The wind began to strengthen during the next two hours. By teatime it was gale force, roaring round the hospital, bashing its westerly wing with a sound like bombs. The sun had gone, and the day was dull. We'll most likely get rain as well, Kate thought, as she left the ward and descended to the ground floor. 'There's a gale warning out, Sister,' the hall porter called, 'up to force ten is imminent, so watch yourself on the coast road. We don't want you blown away, do we? We're short of good-looking Sisters!' Tom Greegan fancied himself as a ladies' man.

Kate fought her way across the car-park, then drove to Morland House, where Rose and her father were saying their goodbyes. Half an hour later they were on their way, with Rose sighing dramatically and complaining about the confines of the car. 'Bob Nansock's Volvo was much more roomy, and this seat-belt is killing me, and you're swaying *all over the road*, Katie!' she squealed as a sudden gust boomed at the car, blowing them off course.

'Sorry, can't help it.' Kate's hands were tight and hard on the wheel. 'We'll be turning soon, we've done the worst,' she shouted above the snarl of the maddened sea as it hit the harbour wall. As they turned up the hill by the Smugglers' Arms, the wind swept the car along like a cockleshell boat under sheets of rain, intermixed with spray. She never knew how she turned in at the gate, got the car into the garage, and herself and Rose safely into the house. They were both breathless, Rose's curly hair was plastered down over her eyes. 'I don't know how you can *bear* to live here!' she burst out fretfully, as Kate dried her hair and made a fuss of her.

'We don't have a gale every day, poppet. This is the first since I've been here.'

'I hate wind!' shuddered Rose.

'Well, I don't suppose anyone actually likes it. It'll blow itself out by morning.' And all I hope is, I'm telling the truth. Kate muttered as she got their supper in a kitchen which felt as though it were under attack.

They ate in the sitting-room, which was fairly quiet, as it faced towards the east. Neither had very much appetite, both felt tense and on edge. 'Only nine more hours and Hugh will be here,' said Rose, as she looked at the clock. 'I wish I could go to bed, I want to be fresh for when he comes.'

'What you mean is you'd like to go upstairs, but you don't fancy your chances under that rattling roof,' said Kate, keeping her voice very light. 'I'll fetch your mattress and you can sleep down here, I'll make up a bed on the floor.'

'Oh, yes, do that. Bring yours down too . . . let's both be here together! I really hate it . . . I'm really frightened . . . I can't be brave like you!' Rose confessed.

'Okay, okay, I'll go and get them.' Kate started for the stairs, and oh dear, how right Rose was! It was very alarming up there. She could hear the roof slates lifting and dropping back like the clatter of plates, the windows strained and creaked and juddered, and the curtains moved in the draught, unidentified scrapings came from the loft. She thumped both mattresses down the stairs, glad to reach the ground floor, then she looked at Rose, then she *saw* Rose, and she felt her heart give a leap. Rose was leaning on the hall table, both hands flat on its top . . . she was rigid, gasping, breathing quickly. Kate moved swiftly towards her.

'I've started the baby . . . I've started, Kate!' gasped Rose, when she could speak. 'I've been having pains since five, but I hoped it might be a false alarm! I don't want it to come . . . I don't want it here . . . I want it at home with Hugh!' She began to sob, putting her arms round Kate's neck. Kate soothed her, smoothing her hair. How could I not have noticed . . . how could I not have seen . . . what sort of a nurse do I think I am? she asked herself. She had blamed the storm for Rose's wan face, for her uneasy fretfulness. She held her sister's hand as another contraction gripped her. Seven minutes since the last one . . . once again it passed. A few tense questions confirmed Kate's fears. 'I don't want my baby in Cornwall!' Rose wailed as her sister reached for the phone.

There was no sound from it. Kate felt sick, as she turned the dial in vain. She had got to get an ambulance. Rose had got to be taken to hospital. She dared not try to take her in the Fiat. The storm raged, Rose gave a cry, but the telephone was mute . . . completely silent, completely uncaring. Kate replaced the receiver and went to Rose, who clung to her, frightened and shocked. 'Rose, there's something wrong with our phone, I'll use the one at Pinnocks. I've got a key, Ellis left me one. I'll ring for an ambulance there.'

'Don't . . . be . . . long!'

'A few minutes—you'll be all right, I promise.' Snatching a mackintosh from the peg and taking the keys from her bag, Kate got the front door open and shut, then drawing on all her courage, braced herself and stepped down from the porch. As the wind drew breath for a second or two, she was able to run a few yards, but the next gust caught her and turned her and hurled her against the cupressus hedge; scratched and shaken, she dropped down on to the ground. But I have to move . . . I have to get up . . . I have got to get into Pinnocks. As she crawled along the sodden ground she found the thin part of the hedge that Ellis used; she scrambled through and, practically on all fours, reached his front door, unlocked it and fell inside. There was the phone . . . oh, blessed phone! Her scratched hand snatched it up. It was then that she groaned. She had no need to dial, there was nothing . . . nothing . . . nothing. The line was dead, the storm must have brought it down.

Kate's mind raced. What should she do? She would have to get help and fast. The nearest telephone from the cottages was down at the Smugglers' Arms. Well, I'll have to get there—I'll have to do it, I'll have to get down that hill, I'll have to get there. I have got to get help for Rose.

She came out of the cottage backwards and hunched, dragging the front door to. Still crouched and moving sideways, she edged her way to the gate. She reached it, opened it, then cried out as the wind snatched it off its hinges and blew it over the hedge like a brown paper kite. She watched it go . . . she couldn't believe it . . . was the whole world blowing to bits? Blinded by rain, her hood jerking back, she grasped the stump of the gate-post, and hung on. It was then that she saw the car. But *was* it a car, or was it a mirage? The rain sheeted over the road, making a screen, then it parted, and there was the car again. It was big and white . . . it was Ian's car! It drew close enough to touch her, its door opened, she was pulled inside, jerked unceremoniously backwards. She rested against him, too breathless to speak, his face was hard on her own, his voice a warm vibration in her ear.

'What were you doing, you crazy girl? What on earth were you doing . . . where were you trying to get to? He moved as she jerked in his arms.

'Ian, it's Rose! She's in labour! I was trying to get to the Inn to get help . . . a taxi or ambulance . . . get her to hospital.'

'I'll take her. I'll get her there.'

'But . . . *can* you?'

'Of course,' Ian smiled at her, and Kate felt a surge of relief. 'I'll get out, come round and help you, then together we'll help Rose.' He opened the door on his side a crack, got through and shut it quickly, sloped his way round the car, and helped Kate out by the hedge. Arms about one another, they ran, and reached the sheltering porch. Seconds later they were in the hall, meeting the lacklustre eyes of a pain-dazed Rose, who said 'Hello, Ian,' in uninterested, unsurprised tones. She had seen him and Kate racing up the path; she had thought when the big white car stopped at the gate that it might be Hugh . . . that Hugh might have got here early, that the car was a taxi. She had thought her husband had come.

Ian took her hand, kissed her cheek. 'Hello, little

Rose. This is a rum way to meet again, after all this time!'

She nodded, but couldn't speak; another contraction was mounting. Through it she heard him saying that the hospital would take good care of her. It wouldn't be long before she was there, and he was going to take her . . . he and Kate. She had nothing to worry about.

Afterwards Kate had only a hazy remembrance of that journey, sitting with Rose in the back of the car, watching the rain-slashed windows, hearing the wind, hearing the sea, thanking God for Ian who was treating the whole thing as run-of-the-mill and driving through the tempestuous evening with a steady calm, permeating confidence.

Rose was admitted into Accident and Emergency, then up to the maternity wards. She was helped into bed in the first-stage room. Kate was told she could stay. She was given a gown and a set of dry clothes, then promising Rose she'd be back, she went down to A and EU in the hope that Ian would still be there. He was, he was talking to Dr Formby. He broke off when he saw Kate. 'You're staying with her, are you?'

'Yes, they say I can. She wants me to.'

'I heard her talk of Hugh's train. When is he due? when is he coming?' asked Ian.

'Tonight—or rather, tomorrow morning. His train gets in at five.'

'I'll meet it, bring him straight here. Now, don't be silly, Kate,' he said quickly, as she tried to stammer her thanks. 'I happen to want to do it. And it's still only half past nine, so I've ample time for some shut-eye before I set off, if I like. It's you who are going to feel on your knees in the morning, I'm afraid.'

'I'm not on duty till one, as it happens,' she told him.

'Well, that's something, I suppose.' She was already

backing away from him, making for the lifts. Her hair
had been strained back into its bun, looking darker as it
was damp. She wore no cap, and the stiff white gown
produced by Sister Hughes stood out from her legs
tent-fashion; she looked clean, and scrubbed, and young
. . . and a little defenceless, which he knew to his cost
she was not.

'Ring your father,' he said abruptly, 'he's worried
about you both. It was he who sent me to your cottage.
I'd seen him at Morland House earlier on, and he was
worried to death, having tried to ring you up and got no
answer. He won't rest till he's spoken to you.'

'I'll ring him before I go into the ward,' Kate promised, and she did so. When her father heard that Rose
was in labour, he nearly went voiceless again. 'You're to
let me know the minute there's any news,' he ordered.

The storm raged until well after midnight, but neither
Kate nor Rose heard it. The only storm Rose was aware
of was the one within her own body. At four a.m. she
was wheeled along into the delivery room. Kate, who
went too, was given a cap and mask. During her midder
course three years ago, she had delivered over thirty
babies. The process of birth was well known to her, but
even so she found that to be a calm and detached
onlooker, when the patient was one's own sister, was a
hard new role and a very daunting one.

Shortly after five-thirty a gowned Hugh Clevington
entered the room and made his way round the obstetric
table. He was recognisable by one or two tufts of recal-
citrant reddish hair sticking out from under his calico
cap. Kate smiled at him as he took her place, up by
Rose's head. Rose knew she was there, but had no time,
nor breath, to do more than acknowledge his presence.
Kate slipped from the room. Her part was done; she
went to the nurses' cloakroom, sluiced her face, and

undid the top of her gown. She stayed in there for several minutes, rubbing her numbed legs, easing her feet in the wooden theatre clogs. Her uniform dress was being dried, the nurses had taken it. Sister Hughes had told her she could have a bed in the Sisters' Residence, and sleep there until her duty time. But she couldn't leave the maternity floor until Rose's baby was born. She opened the door and went into the corridor, and sat down on a form. At the far end, by the entrance doors, she saw Ian approaching—refreshed and smiling, impeccably dressed. I don't know how he does it, passed through her mind, as he sat down by her side. 'How's it going?' he asked. 'Any news yet?'

'Not yet, but it shouldn't be long.' She turned her head and met his smile, drowned in his glance and smiled back. How long have I loved him . . . how long, how long . . . perhaps in another world, she thought. But what nonsense, what fantasy! 'How wonderful,' she said, 'that you got Hugh here, and in time too. It'll mean so much to Rose.' Her voice trailed off; she was very, very tired.

'Kate darling, you ought to rest.'

'Once the baby's come.' The endearment, the effect it had, made her close her eyes in case he should see what showed there . . . all he was being was kind. I have *consciously* loved him since the night of the party, that stuffy consultants' party, when Helen appeared and bore him off, like one of the waiting wives. Quickly, nervously, she began to ask him how Helen's mother was. 'Whatever must you think of me for not asking before?'

'There hasn't been much opportunity, has there?' Ian looked up and smiled, as one of the nursing auxiliaries handed a cup of tea to each of them, then disappeared kitchenwards. Each saucer held two lumps of sugar, and

Ian stirred his in. 'Mrs Reever is very ill,' he said, 'she's out of danger now, but she'll need a great deal of care for some time. She has a spinal injury, the extent of which isn't yet fully known.'

'Oh dear, I'm so sorry, and how dreadful for Helen!'

He nodded, his face serious. 'The Carringtons are with her now. When they arrived I came home. I promised Nell I'd see Miss Norton, ask her if she'd be willing to go to Boston and look after Mrs Reever, when she comes out of hospital.'

'She'll jump at it.' Kate shifted a little on the hard wooden form. 'When I saw her she was bemoaning the fact that she hadn't got a passport. I'm sure once she got . . .' She stopped short at that point, for she had seen Hugh approaching. He was smiling so much that his ginger moustache seemed to stretch from ear to ear.

'We have a son . . . a little boy . . . a perfect little boy! Rose is fine, they're taking her down to the post-natal ward. The baby's being cleaned up, he's a red-faced, yelling six-pounder!' Kate hardly knew him, he was so excited; he kissed her and swung her round. Ian and he shook hands and they slapped one another on the back. Breaches were healed with abandon and relish, hard feelings flew out of the window. Ian kissed Kate, holding her tightly, crushing her calico gown.

'Congratulations, Aunt Kate!' he whispered, while Hugh looked on. Two of the delivery room nurses joined them, and they all stood there in a group, laughing and talking, forgetting their tiredness, and drinking the baby's health in hospital tea . . . hot and sweet and strong.

It was seven a.m. when they left the hospital. Ian was taking Hugh home to Tolcanbury Close for breakfast. Kate was bound for the Sisters' Home. They escorted her there, across the courtyard, while the brand-new

morning fell about them in clear-washed light, scoured
by the recent storm. Puffball clouds sailed high against a
sky of peerless blue; the breeze was no more than a
whispering promise of the summer's day to come. 'Get
some sleep, Kate,' Ian said, as they left her in the hall.
But first she had to ring her mother, and she crossed to
the line of kiosks. Hugh was telling her father, he would
see him at Morland House before Ian discharged him
after lunch.

Audrey Christy was having her breakfast when Kate's
call came through. She said she was not in the least
surprised that Rose had given birth while still in Cornwall, but through the cool blasé-ness of her voice Kate
sensed her pleasure. 'So now I'm a grandmother!' Her
laugh was half a sigh.

'A glamorous one,' Kate assured her. It was her turn
to heave a sigh. 'Mother, I simply have to go—I'm dead
on my feet. I've been up all night and . . .'

'Kate, I've decided to marry Edward.' The quick, bald
statement jerked Kate to attention; she knew she was
pleased at the news.

'Oh, Mummy, I'm glad, I'm so glad! I'd been thinking
about what you said, about yourself and Mr Jules, when
we said goodbye, last week. I know you'll be happy, I
just know you will—I feel it in my bones!'

'Thank you, darling . . . bless you for that!' The short
following silence was emotionally charged, and Kate
saw the little posse of Sisters who were passing the
kiosks, through a moving blur. 'You can tell your father
and Rose, if you like,' her mother's voice started again.
'On second thoughts, though, perhaps not today . . .
today belongs to Rose and Hugh and the baby. I may
ring your father tonight.'

Later, in the borrowed room up on the second floor,
Kate tried to sleep, but found it hard; there was so much

to think about. It was only when she gave up trying that drowsiness encroached, dimming the memory of a laughing Ian calling her 'Aunt Kate'; it dimmed the feel of his mouth on hers . . . mercifully made more dim the realisation that his thoughts were for Helen, with her mother in Massachusetts. When Miss Norton went out there, Helen was sure to return.

CHAPTER TWELVE

KATE saw her nephew for the first time during her tea-break that day. He lay in his crib beside Rose, eyes blue as cornflowers; Rose was all smiles, sitting up, holding Hugh's hand. Her father and Maxine were there, but the two little boys had been left at Newquay in the care of the hotel's child minder service. They enjoyed this, they liked the organised games.

'Ian's got Hugh booked into the City Hotel,' said Rose. 'He's staying there until Friday—we go home Friday night, we can't wait to get back to Highgate with our son.' She smiled at Hugh, and he at her, and the others felt de trop. Kate looked at the baby, bending low to his crib.

'I could stand and stare at you for ever,' she told him quietly, putting one of her fingers into his starfish hand. Danny had never wanted a child—'Let's keep it just you and me', had been his response when Kate had brought the baby subject up. She had gone along with what he said, not worrying overmuch; they were young and in time Danny would change his mind. Maxine touched her arm, breaking into her thoughts.

'We'll run you home this evening, Kate, when you come off duty. John and I are eating here in Tradstow. We can pick you up at half-eight.'

'We certainly can,' John Christy put in. 'I'm a free man now. I can do as I please.' He threw up his hands, as Ian pushed through the curtains. 'Ah, here's my one-time jailer, I'd better watch what I say!'

'You're allowed to run your daughter home, sir!' Ian

kissed Rose's cheek, and admired the baby. 'Well done! He's a lovely specimen.'

'Dine with us, Ian.' Maxine looked at him. 'You've been so wonderful. Kate was telling us what you did last night, driving all through that storm.'

'Storms are my speciality, Mrs Christy!' Ian smiled. 'Thank you for the invitation, but I've got a phone call coming through from America round about eight o'clock. I must be at home to answer it.'

'What about tomorrow night?' John Christy broke in. 'Damn it, we've got to celebrate the birth of my first grandchild! How about you and Kate joining Maxie and me for a meal? We'll go to the Majestic . . . Hugh, you must come as well.'

'I shall be here with Rose, thanks, John,' Hugh Clevington said, delighting Rose, who had been on the point of refusing on his behalf. Hugh and she would celebrate on their own.

'I would like to come very much indeed,' Kate heard Ian say. His tone was affable, even effusive, but she felt, nevertheless, that her father by his very enthusiasm had put him in a position where, without being churlish, he could hardly refuse again.

She left the ward soon after this, and returned to her duties. Ian went back to the Royal Clinic, accompanied by Hugh, who wanted to see what building improvements were envisaged. Hugh was a man with look-ahead ideas.

'Was it bad at the cottage last night, Kate?' enquired Maxine, as they drove out to Poldenack just before nine p.m.

'Hair-raising . . . literally!' Kate, in the back of the Rolls, comfortable and half asleep, yawned and opened her eyes. 'But it sounded worse than it was, I think. There was certainly plenty of noise!'

'You sound as though you need plenty of sleep.'

'I haven't caught up with it yet.' She yawned again, and dozed for the next two miles. She was awake, though, when they took the hill and cruised along the lane. She stared at her cottage, at the roof in particular . . . not one slate was missing, nor out of place. She could hardly believe her eyes. The chimneys were upright, the windows were in; only the battered garden, and Ellis's gate at the foot of a tree, bore witness to the fact that a gale had ever ravaged them at all. Her gaze went next door, and it was then that she saw Ellis's blue Cortina. 'Why, he's back!' she cried. 'Ellis is back . . . *just* back, by the looks of it.' The boot was open, which probably meant he had been unloading it.

'I'm glad he is. I don't like to think of you all by yourself up here,' her father said, as they trooped into the house.

'And even the phone's back on now.' Kate lifted the receiver, putting it back as she heard the dialling tone. The mattresses lying on the stairs were irrefutable testimony to the girls' fright the night before; John Christy and his wife got them back to the bedrooms, while Maxine made Kate's bed.

'Now get in it, darling, and have a good night.' She kissed Kate and went downstairs. She and John left soon afterwards, but as they reached the car, Ellis appeared and intercepted them. They stood chatting for several minutes, and the sound of their voices drifted up to Kate as she kicked off her shoes and began to undress. She supposed she ought to go out and join them; it seemed awfully rude to Ellis to skulk in here, and not say, 'welcome back'. In the end, though, she decided to save her greetings for the morrow, for surely Ellis, after the drag of the journey from London, would rather she didn't crowd him on his first night.

She surmised wrongly, for a few seconds after the car had left the gate, she saw him coming up her path, lanky and blurred in the dusk. She slipped on a robe and went to meet him, and he stepped in as she opened the door. 'Hello, Kate,' he smiled.

'Hello, Ellis . . . good to see you back.'

'I won't keep you long. Your father said you were just turning in.' He perched on a stool, he was wearing dark trousers and a cream silk shirt. He also sported a tie, which gave him an unfamiliar look.

'How was the trip?' she asked him. She fetched lager from the fridge, and a Coke for herself; it might help to keep her awake.

Ellis told her a little about his meetings with his publishers and agent. 'They have asked to see the first half of my current novel,' he said. 'I have to work closely with them on this one, so I'm going back to London, to finish it. I'm giving the cottage up.'

'Oh, Ellis, what a pity!' Kate was sorry. She had grown very accustomed to him being next door, she didn't want that to change. Yet during the time he had been away, had she really thought much about it, about *him*? She knew she had not. Once Rose had arrived she hardly noticed the absence of noise from Pinnocks, nor missed the sight of Ellis moving about. I like him . . . *very* much, she thought, but his company is the kind one can take or leave, and she felt so mean about having these kind of thoughts that she made him a sandwich, one of the strong cheese sort.

'You've been good to me.' He ate the sandwich in the neat, quick way she remembered. 'And I would like you to know that I really have appreciated your kindness.'

'That sounds like a goodbye speech,' she laughed. 'When are you actually leaving?'

He leaned across to the draining-board, clattering his

plate on the top. 'Tomorrow, as soon as it's light. I'll be gone before you get up.'

'I see, so it really *is* goodbye.'

Ellis nodded and stared at his knees. He looked like a man who felt there was something else he ought to say, but was unable to find the right words, which couldn't be true in his case. Writers were never lost for words, so he must be afraid to say them. Kate got to her feet and ended his misery.

'Well, it just remains for me to wish you luck, doesn't it, Ellis, and to say how much I've enjoyed your company. I'm so glad we met. I wish you all success with your writing, and I'll be watching *Bland Justice* on the square box, as from November on. I expect you're glad Father's better?' She added this deliberately. She had never forgotten how cursory he had been when Pa was ill.

'Of course I am, I like your father,' was the stiff reply she got. Shortly after that he left; Kate stood at the kitchen door, watched him push his way through the hedge and cross the lawn to his cottage . . . for the very last time . . . and then she went to bed.

On the following day, Wednesday, William Jarman's theatre list was a lengthy one, and the two main wards —Penhallow and Fratton—were kept at full stretch, not helped by the fact that a nurse was on leave from each. Olly was without his staff nurse, Kate was without Nurse Heston, Pat Finn, whom they shared, had gone to the Neuro Wing. Olly looked hot and miserable when he met Kate on the landing. They met in a criss-cross passing fashion, so there was no time to talk. There was time for lunch, but only just; Kate had a tray in her office. She was sifting her way through a limp salad when Ian made an appearance. He looked at her plate and raised an eyebrow. 'I don't approve of that. You ought to get off the ward to eat, and relax for half an hour.

'He's quite right, Kate.' Hugh followed him in. He had spent the morning with Ian. He had watched him perform a laryngectomy, had been willing to assist. It was like old times, with roles reversed; the operating team at the ENT Clinic had been suitably impressed.

Ian had called to see Mrs Colton; he had authorised her discharge the day before, and he wanted to say goodbye. He repaired to the day room to do just that, Hugh went up to see Rose, while Kate finished her lunch and began on her paperwork. Ian came out of the ward just as the porters from theatre were wheeling Mrs Albertson who had had a spleen operation, back to her bed inside the doors. Kate left her office and followed them in, and Ian passed close enough to whisper: 'See you this evening,' into her ear. This evening was her father's small dinner party at the stately Majestic Hotel. In a way she was looking forward to it, but she thought it might be sticky, because did Ian *really* want to come?

They all four met in the plush red, white and gold cocktail lounge at seven-thirty. Kate was the last to arrive. She was wearing a dark rose-pink dress in heavy crisp cotton, with a swirling skirt and a flounce round the scooped out neck. Her hair was down and left loose to lie in swathes on her shoulders. Heads turned as she walked across the room. Her father swelled with pride when he saw her. 'You're late, but you're worth waiting for!' he smiled.

'Pink suits you, Kate.' Maxine, in drifty lilac chiffon, smiled at her from behind her Pimms Number One.

Ian endorsed both remarks, as he held out a chair for Kate. His black velvet jacket set off his fairness, his eyes under straight, thick brows were unfathomable. Kate felt shy of him.

Over an excellent meal in the L-shaped dining-room, the conversation, led by John Christy, ranged from politics to investments, from plays running in the West End to books and television. Finally it got round to marriage and babies, and a solemn toast was drunk to Justin Mark, Rose and Hugh's little son. 'I'm a grandpa, damn it,' groaned John. 'Makes me feel proud, but old. It makes our two youngsters step-uncles at the ages of seven and five!' He looked at Maxine, who laughed at him.

'And it makes me a step-grandma!' She looked so young to be one that they all convulsed with laughter.

'My ex-wife's getting married again,' said John, turning to Ian. Marrying her partner at the end of October. He's got two teenage grandchildren. So now you can work out what relation they'll be to young Justin! Oh, Kate,' he broke off, 'while I think of it, did Ellis see you last night?'

'Yes, he did, to say goodbye. He went back to London this morning. He has to work closely with his publishers.'

'He's going back to his wife.' There was a small silence, and Kate put down her fork. 'Surely he told you, darling?' Struck by the look on his daughter's face, John cursed the weakness of men like Ellis Rand who seldom faced up to things.

'He most certainly didn't tell me!' Kate said indignantly. She was aware of the movement of Ian's arm as he raised his coffee cup. 'I had no idea he was married,' she said. Her father pursed his lips.

'Well, he is . . . to a nursing Sister at the London Hospital. They've been living apart for some years—she took a post in Saudi. Now she's back at the London, and back with Ellis. He wants Maxie and me to meet her. He's a funny chap in some respects . . . clever, but secretive.'

'He's entitled to his secrets,' shrugged Kate.

'Depends what they are, I think.' John looked troubled; all he hoped was that Kate was uninvolved. Not that he thought Rand was her type; he flicked a glance at Ian, who was drinking his coffee with a face like granite. He sighed and called the waiter . . . you never knew where you were with young people these days.

Soon after that the party broke up, saying good night in the foyer. Kate was going home by taxi, Bob Nansock had brought her in, and was driving her home—the arrangement being that she would ring him up as soon as she was ready to leave the hotel. 'I'll wait with you till he comes,' said Ian, 'or you might get abducted . . . borne off, never to be seen again.'

'This is Tradstow, not the Arabian Desert!'

'But sheiks abound here as well!' And sure enough, emerging from the dining-room were six Middle-Eastern gentlemen in the headdress and robes of the country from whence they came.

Kate telephoned Bob and was told by his father that he hadn't got back from Porthcothan. 'He got held up, Mrs Browning. I'm afraid it'll be an hour at least before he gets out to you.'

'I'll wait in the foyer.' Kate hung up and went back to Ian. She explained what had happened:

'Go and get your coat and we'll stroll down to the quay. It's a fine night, it'll do us good.' He flicked a glance at his watch.

'But do you want to wait that long?'

'Yes.' His tone was terse . . . it was his ordering voice, and Kate did as she was told. 'You were shocked when you heard about Rand, weren't you?' he said, as they walked down the steps on to the quay with its wide stone paving slabs. It was twilight, and the breeze off the water smelled of tar, and rope, and rusty chains; it streamed Kate's hair out behind.

'I don't like being lied to.' She was slightly ahead of him, a white wraith in her mohair coat, with loose wide sleeves.

'Being lied to is very demeaning.'

'Yes.' She thought how true that was. And Ellis had lied, he had acted a lie, had posed as a single man. He had told her he had never tried marriage, then changed the subject cleverly, like a smooth transition from one scene to the next. He had told his readers he was unattached, but no doubt, just as adroitly, he would be able to think of something to cover that. 'I just think it was dishonest,' she said, trying to hold her hair flat.

'He may not have looked upon it as lying, more as poetic licence!'

'Oh, rubbish!' she snapped, and was unaware of how like her mother she sounded.

'Did you care for him?' Ian stared out over the estuary. Three rivers converged at Tradstow, where the viaduct over the valley looked high enough to hang from the darkening sky. Kate moved at his side.

'No,' she said, 'there was nothing like that . . . not so much as a spark. I didn't know who he was till I'd been at the cottage some weeks. Then we got to speaking, and when he found out whose daughter I was, he seemed to want to be friendly . . . I did too, in a way. I liked cooking for him, and having him round, and helping him all I could, but we didn't attract one another—not in a sexual way.'

'I find that very hard to believe,' said Ian.

She was furious when he said that. And yet—and yet—who could blame him for being sceptical? Each time he had come to Aubyns Ellis had been there, looking at home, looking entrenched, and it *had* been a strange quirk of fate that brought him to live right next door to her. Still, she couldn't keep on explaining, and neither was it his business. 'You'll have to believe what you like,' she said quietly, hearing the shake in her voice.

'Kate!' She felt his arm thread through hers, felt his fingers encircling her wrist. The movement brought her close to his side, their legs moved in unison—hip-to-hip, thigh-to-thigh. I shall love him till I die, soared through her mind, while a feeling of anguish and hopelessness heavied her limbs. Ian belonged to Helen, all he was doing was passing the time with her, passing the time until Helen got back from the States. And I ought to have more sense than to be walking down here with him, so why don't I just turn round and go back? she thought. Why is he questioning me? Finding the strength on a peak of anger, she wrenched her arm free of his grip. 'I just find it hard,' he said slowly, not attempting to touch her again, 'that Rand didn't want to make love to you, situated as you were.'

'Well, he didn't. I'm not a green girl. A woman can always tell. I liked him, or thought I did, now I'm not even sure about that. He's talented, and he should do well, he's clever and will forge ahead, especially with someone beside him, with a *wife* to look after him. All Ellis needs is permanent back-up help.'

'You believe in marriage, do you?'

'It doesn't suit everyone,' she said evasively.

'Did it suit you?'

'Yes, mine was happy,' Kate smiled, and he saw her relax. 'Everyone said it wouldn't be, everyone warned me against it—I was too young at eighteen, they said, and Danny would never settle. Danny and I won our happiness, we adjusted to one another, we pulled together, we became a partnership. When he died I felt deserted, wronged, even bitter, I suppose. All I wanted during those first awful weeks of widowhood was to marry again, to be one of a pair. I felt utterly wrong being single. Pretty soon after that I went to the other end of the pole; I wanted to stand on my own, I wanted to be my own person—to fulfil myself in my nursing career.'

'Thank you for telling me,' Ian said quietly.

'You asked.'

'Yes.' They stood at the end of the quay. Clear in his mind was a scene in his garden, nearly three months ago when, snatching herself from his arms, she had told him . . . oh, so very plainly . . . that she liked her life exactly as it was.

'We'd better go back,' he heard her say now.

'Yes, I suppose we had.' As they turned they saw the entwined couple standing by the ramp—a pair of lovers, lost to the world. Kate averted her eyes. On a burst of embarrassment, and more for something to say than anything else, she began to talk about Rose and the baby.

'I'm to be godmother,' she told Ian in high falsetto tones.

He made some kind of grunting comment; she thrust her hands into her pockets, dragging down her loose wool coat and turning to look at him. In the half-light, so nearly dark, he showed up in silhouette—a sharply defined cut-out against a backcloth of water and bobbing lights and night sky of scudding clouds.

'Did it feel awkward meeting Rose and Hugh again?' The temerity of her question appalled her, as soon as it left her lips. Her relief when she saw his face ruck in a smile made her let out her breath in a rush.

'You mean, did I want to punch Hugh on the nose, and did old feelings kindle for Rose? No, Kate, to both of those.'

'You loved Rose once,' she reminded him.

'Not nearly enough . . . as later events were to prove. Rose showed sense beyond her years in breaking things off between us. It was the manner of the breaking that got me, I was angered rather than hurt. Like you, I don't like being lied to, and your sister and the Prof acted a lie for a very long time before the truth emerged. I'm glad things have worked out for them. I'm hoping they'll work out for me.'

'I'm sure they will, once Helen gets back.' Kate made herself say the words, and once again their boldness shocked her. Was it the wine or the darkness that was giving her the courage to delve so deep?

'You think so?'

'Of course,' she smiled, while a terrible bleakness dropped like a shroud over her shoulders. She shivered, and hugged herself. 'Once she gets back from the States, and her mother starts to get well . . .'

Ian steadied her as she lurched on a slippery patch of cobbles. Holding her elbow, he steered her to a seat hewn out of stone, and they sat there, shoulders touching. I can't move, she thought. I can't move, I must have this . . . this very last time with him. I must have this, she can't grudge me this. She felt him touch her hair, moving it like a curtain over her face.

'My happiness doesn't lie with Nell. How can you think it does?' He swept her hair back and turned her, making her look at him. 'How can you think it does . . . how *can* you?' Their faces were inches apart.

'You went to America, and you always seemed . . . you always seemed attached.' Her voice came throatily, thick with emotion.

'You've been listening to gossip, Kate. Nell and I were close for a time, soon after I came down here, but the affair ended six months ago, perfectly amicably. There was no ill-feeling when it was done, just the bonus of a friendship, which in spite of what the cynics say, was well worth having.'

'I didn't realise . . . I always thought . . .' She couldn't think at all, not when he was as near as this, not when their breath was mingling, not when he was touching her face, cradling the back of her head, drawing her closer, gravely kissing her lips.

'Will you ever get round to wanting to be one of a pair again?' Ian asked. 'Are you still grieving for Daniel?'

She laid her face on his. 'He was once my dear, dear love, but I don't long for him now. Danny belongs to my past.'

He kissed her eyes, and felt the tears squeezing from under her lids. 'I love you, Kate . . . you know that, don't you?' He made her look at him, and she saw the pale thickness of his brows, the proud bridge of his nose, the level mouth forming wonderful words—words she ached to hear. 'I never knew I had it in me to love a woman so much.'

And she had never loved a man so much . . . to love so much was frightening. 'I thought you just wanted me, that's all,' she told him.

'*Just* . . . and that's *all*!' His hand gripped hers. 'Of course, of course I want you! I was attracted to you the first time I met you, and I know what you're going to say—that I was engaged to Rose then, and you were married to Daniel, but even so, that was the way it was. I never forgot you, either, you stayed in my mind like a dream. When I walked on to your ward that day, all those weeks ago, when I saw you there, I couldn't believe it. I was knocked sideways, stunned. Later, when I learned that Daniel had died, I wanted to look after you. I think I began to love you from that time on. I knew I loved you that night in my garden, when I held you in my arms. You were pliant and sweet and very loving, then you fled and told me off. I felt less than the dust, reduced to nothing. Even then I didn't give up, not entirely, not until I saw Ellis Rand at your cottage, and assumed you and he had formed a relationship. Do you love me at all?' His voice dropped in cadence. It was little more than a whisper.

'With all my heart,' she said simply. But could this really be true? Could it be true? Was it really happening, or was it part of a dream—a glorious dream from which she would soon awake?

'It is true . . . it's really true . . . it's happening, my love!' Ian said as he got to his feet and folded her in his arms.

'How did you know?' Kate asked softly.

'What you were thinking? I don't *always* know,' he smiled, 'but I did then, perhaps because I feel the awe of it too . . . that you and I should come together . . . *you* and *I*, Kate, after all this time, and through so much! When will you marry me?'

'Soon . . . soon, as soon as you like!' She laced her arms round his neck. She could feel the beat of his heart against hers, the hardness of his face, the rough-soft masculine skin, the seeking of his lips as they gentled hers before their kiss took fire. Time stood still, then raced away on stormy wings of love, which bore them off, bore them aloft, leaving the world behind. Yet with it all, along with it all, along with the joy of it all, was a deep sense of rightness and safety . . . a feeling of coming home . . .

And they knew they would love one another all their lives.

The comments of the family were varied, but Kate knew they would be. Getting engaged to the man who had once been engaged to your sister was bound to cause eyebrows to be raised. Hugh Clevington's comment was: 'Well, I'm blessed!' Rose jerked her chin. 'I could see it coming a mile off,' she declared, but she kissed them and wished them luck. John Christy was delighted, and so was Maxine. Kate's mother said she was pleased, but involved in plans for her own wedding, she was just a shade lukewarm. 'Mummy's pretty cool about most things,' Kate explained to Ian. His own parents weren't, they were overjoyed. 'We're so glad about it, my dear!' They had met Kate before, just briefly, when they had come to the Surrey house, two and a half years ago. They had thought Rose very lightweight, a charming girl, but not right for their son. Kate was perfect, she had strength and purpose, she had a straight look to her eye. Ian's father, who was a rural dean, promised to marry them at the little church at Poldenack Bay on the twenty-ninth of September. The six weeks up until then were busy ones.

Helen Reever came back from Boston a month before the wedding. Ian and Kate met her at Miss Norton's house one evening. Both Helen and Miss Norton were congratulatory, but they, too, were deep in plans. After they had put the sale of the shop and Norty's house in hand, they were going out to America: 'For good and all,' Helen said. 'Boston has always fascinated me, I'd have gone there long ago, had it not been for *other* fascinations.' She looked straight at Ian then, while Kate stared at the floor. Miss Norton blew her nose. 'I'm starting a business out there,' Helen went on breezily. 'Norty and I will live with Mother, the house is as big as a barn. She'll be able to walk in time, they say, but it's going to be a long job.' She looked sad for a moment, then brightened again. 'Are you going to keep on working after you and Ian are married, Kate?'

'For a time, yes,' Kate told her.

'Till you start a family, I suppose? I hope you'll be happy. We all have to live the kind of life we want, or strive for it.' Helen gave a little laugh.

On the night before her wedding Kate removed Danny's ring. She put it in a little box and put the box in one of her drawers. She looked at the mark on her finger, which tomorrow would be covered by a brand-new ring, by Ian's ring. 'I love him, Danny,' she said. 'I can't be happy without him, and that's the way of it.' Standing at her window, she looked out at the night, and she thanked whoever had brought her to this new beginning . . . to this new chance of happiness.

The burning secrets of a girl's first love.

She was young and rebelliou fighting the restrictions im posed by her South America convent.

He was a doctor, dedicate to the people of his war-tor country.

Drawn together by sensual attraction. Nothin should have stood in their wa

Yet a tragic secret was keep them apart …

Following Hidden in th Flame's tremendous succe last year here's another chan to read this passionate story.

Mills & Boon

4 Doctor Nurse Romances
FREE

Coping with the daily tragedies and ordeals of a busy hospital, and sharing the satisfaction of a difficult job well done, people find themselves unexpectedly drawn together. Mills & Boon Doctor Nurse Romances capture perfectly the excitement, the intrigue and the emotions of modern medicine, that so often lead to overwhelming and blissful love. By becoming a regular reader of Mills & Boon Doctor Nurse Romances you can enjoy SIX superb new titles every two months plus a whole range of special benefits: your very own personal membership card, a free newsletter packed with recipes, competitions, bargain book offers, plus big cash savings.

**AND an Introductory FREE GIFT for YOU.
Turn over the page for details.**

Fill in and send this coupon back today
and we'll send you
4 Introductory
Doctor Nurse Romances yours to keep
FREE
At the same time we will reserve a
subscription to Mills & Boon
Doctor Nurse Romances for you. Every
two months you will receive the latest
6 new titles, delivered direct to your door.
You don't pay extra for delivery. Postage and
packing is always completely Free.
There is no obligation or commitment –
you receive books only for
as long as you want to.

It's easy! Fill in the coupon below and return it to
**MILLS & BOON READER SERVICE, FREEPOST, P.O. BOX 236,
CROYDON, SURREY CR9 9EL.**

Please note: READERS IN SOUTH AFRICA write to
Independent Books Services P.T.Y.,
Postbag X3010, Randburg 2125, S. Africa

- -